I0822165

THE FOURTH REICH

—REBORN—

The Fourth Reich Reborn

ISBN: 979-8-9893424-3-3 (hardback)
979-8-9893424-2-6 (paperback)

Printed in the United States of America

THE FOURTH REICH

—REBORN—

A Jeannie Loomis Novel

with Sean Delaney

GARY J. ROSE

To my beloved Mom, who was the first to read the unpublished manuscript of "The Fourth Reich." I have no doubt that she, along with Dad, watches over me as I pen this sequel.

To my dear sister, who now meticulously proofreads my manuscript, uncovering errors I might have missed. Your keen eye is invaluable, and I'm grateful for your support.

To Gill McDonald for another great editing job. You always make my novels better.

And to all my devoted Jeannie Loomis fans, your heartfelt reviews serve as the driving force behind my writing. Your encouragement keeps me inspired to continue this journey.

THE FOURTH REICH REBORN

A Jeannie Loomis novel
With the return of Interpol Agent
Sean Delaney

SS OATH OF ALLEGIANCE

"I swear by God this holy oath that I shall render unconditional obedience to the Leader of the German Reich and people, Adolf Hitler, supreme commander of the armed forces, and that as a brave soldier I shall at all times be prepared to give my life for this oath."

OTHER JEANNIE LOOMIS THRILLER NOVELS:

Ark of the Covenant – Raid on the Church of Our Lady Mary of Zion

Star Chamber

Forgotten Plans

House of Special Purpose

Time Game

The Fourth Reich

Black Heart/Black Cell

The Phantom Train

Rollercoaster

Snow Angel

OTHER BOOKS BY THE AUTHOR:

Horror/Sci-fi

House on Haunted Hill Resurrection

Beneath the Earth

The Tingler Unleashed

Carnival of Lost Souls

SEAL – Ghost Recon

Non-Fiction

Towards the Integration of Police Psychology Techniques to Combat Juvenile Delinquency in K-12 Schools

Hitting Rock Bottom

Teaching Inside the Walls

How to Create a Public-School Military-Style Boot Camp Academy

A NOTE TO READERS

With the overwhelming success of my novel *The Fourth Reich,* published in 2021, which left my readers pondering the fate of the missing Hitler clone, I find myself convinced that now is the perfect time for its thrilling sequel. I want to express my deepest gratitude for your kind reviews, not only for *The Fourth Reich* but also for all the other Jeannie Loomis thrillers, as well as my five horror books, *House on Haunted Hill Resurrection*, *Beneath the Earth*, *The Tingler Unleashed*, *Carnival of Lost Souls*, and *SEAL – Ghost Recon*.

Reviews are the lifeblood we writers yearn for as, contrary to popular belief, there's not a substantial financial gain in publishing a book unless you possess a massive platform, an extensive Internet following, or unlimited funds to invest in publishing and promotional firms for name recognition.

Personally, I rely on the incredible support of my fans through word-of-mouth recommendations to potential readers, along with occasional updates about the upcoming release of my next novel. It is thanks to you that many of my novels have achieved the top

10% ranking within their genre, and for that, I am eternally grateful. Your unwavering encouragement and enthusiasm keep me motivated to continue crafting stories that captivate and enthrall you.

"THE FOURTH REICH" - A RECAP

Let's revisit the gripping world of *The Fourth Reich*, where the plot unraveled an intricate and chilling conspiracy that kept readers on the edge of their seats.

In this electrifying tale, young women in their early twenties with striking physical similarities - blond hair, blue eyes, and athletic builds - were mysteriously vanishing in Europe, with a few unfortunate souls taken in the United States. Little did the world know that 'The Organization,' a sinister group of modern-day Nazis descended from SS officers, was behind these horrifying abductions.

Operating under the guidance of a relative of the infamous Angel of Death, Dr. Joseph Mengele, 'The Organization' delved into nightmarish genetic experiments. Their audacious plan involved stealing Hitler's remains from the FSB in Moscow, intending to use the Führer's DNA for a terrifying purpose.

Enter FBI agent Jeannie Loomis, a strong and dedicated law enforcement officer on a drive to confront her essential flaw: a struggle with blackouts due to excessive drinking and waking up next to strangers. While investigating the missing women, Jeannie and her team, with the assistance of agent Sean Delaney from Interpol, initially believed they were dealing with an international sex trafficking ring.

However, as the investigation progressed, they uncovered Dr. Hausser's sinister activities at a secluded hospital on an island off the coast of South America. The horrifying truth emerged - the kidnapped young women were being used as surrogate mothers to create Adolf Hitler clones.

In a heart-stopping turn of events, Jeannie herself became a victim when she was kidnapped and taken to the secluded island. While Agent Delaney and his team staged a raid on the compound, they narrowly missed capturing the doctor and Jeannie. Dr. Hausser had already distributed several Hitler clones to SS officers, hoping they would be raised to maturity so he could determine which one most closely resembled the actual Adolf Hitler while eliminating the rest.

Ultimately, the doctor and his trusted nurse absconded with one of the clones, relocating to Hitler's hometown to further their terrifying plan. Agent Delaney tirelessly pursued the doctor and Jeannie, and, in a fierce gun battle, the doctor accidentally killed the clone while being eliminated by Delaney. The nurse took her own life with a cyanide capsule.

Wounded but resolute, Jeannie persevered through the ordeal, and the whereabouts of all the clones were accounted for... except one. And so, the first *Fourth Reich* novel concluded, leaving an enigmatic and haunting question unanswered.

THE STAND-ALONE NATURE OF THE SEQUEL

As we embark on the sequel, it's important to note that, as with all Jeannie Loomis thriller novels, this one stands on its own, ready to captivate readers anew. While the events of the first *Fourth Reich* novel significantly shaped Jeannie's character and journey, the sequel introduces fresh challenges and mysteries, taking us on an adrenaline-pumping ride with unexpected twists and turns.

Whether you're a devoted Jeannie Loomis fan or a new reader intrigued by this thrilling world, rest assured that the sequel's narrative is complete in itself. As Jeannie faces her next set of trials, the story unfolds independently while still preserving the heart-pounding excitement that defines the Jeannie Loomis series.

Thank you for being a part of this incredible journey; I'm truly grateful for your unwavering support. So, without further ado, let's dive into the next chapter of Jeannie Loomis' extraordinary life and unravel the mysteries that lie ahead. Let the adventure begin.

ONE

SOUTHEAST GERMAN TOWN OF BERCHTESGADEN

An eerie shadow crept over the infamous structure known in English as the Eagle's Nest as dusk descended upon the Kehlsteinhaus. Perched atop the summit of the Kehlstein, a rugged outcrop looming above Obersalzberg near the southeastern German town of Berchtesgaden, the Nazi-constructed edifice, with its chilling history, was a haunting reminder of the dark days of the past. Reserved solely for high-ranking members of the Nazi Party, it served as a clandestine venue for government affairs and social gatherings.

As night continued falling over the Eagle's Nest, the imposing structure stood defiantly atop the sheer rock wall as a testament to the Nazi regime's audacity. Despite the destruction of many Nazi buildings after World War II, this edifice remained untouched, reigning proudly over the once impassable terrain, its golden brass elevator hidden deep within the mountain symbolizing a climb to the "summit of power." A feat of architectural brilliance, it was, nonetheless, a wasteful affront to nature and resources, designed to impress and awe with its grandeur.

Despite its dark history, the building became a legend in the postwar era, featuring prominently in popular U.S. war films and series. Undamaged and surviving as one of the few monuments from Hitler's time, it gained an undeserved prominence, eliciting both fascination and unease. Berchtesgaden, the town below, has long outlasted its political significance, but the Eagle's Nest lingers as a haunting reminder of an idyllic facade designed to overshadow the horrors of a sinister era.

Originally conceived by Martin Bormann, the Eagle's Nest remarkably survived the Allied bombings during the war, thanks in part to the intervention of former Governor Jacob. After 1960, when Berchtesgaden was incorporated into Bavaria, the Bavarian government relinquished control of the building, entrusting it to a charitable trust and directing its proceeds toward benevolent causes, or so it appeared to the public.

Yet, tonight, amid the tranquility and charitable façade, an ominous event would unfold, a momentous occasion in the resurrection of the Nazi empire. Adolf Hitler's missing clone, kept secret until now, would make his fateful appearance at the mountaintop retreat, shrouding the night in uncertainty and foreboding. The echoes of history seemed to stir as if warning of the potential consequences that lay ahead.

Unbeknownst to most Bavarians, the charitable image projected by the Eagle's Nest was a mere illusion—a mask veiling a sinister reality. Behind the façade of benevolence, The Organization, a clandestine international group of modern-day Nazis, secretly owned the Eagle's Nest. And tonight, they were about to stage a momentous event—a pivotal step in the rebirth of the Nazi Party.

Winter had cast its icy grip upon the region, and the Eagle's Nest, now transformed into a popular tourist attraction, lay dormant, its doors closed until the reopening scheduled for May 12, 2023. The surrounding snow-laden roads made travel treacherous, but some vehicles managed to cautiously navigate the mountainous terrain at reduced speeds. Among them, seven black Mercedes made their way up the road, nearing the entrance to the tunnel that housed the renowned elevator leading to the historic site.

As the moon ascended above the snow-capped peaks, casting an eerie glow over the mountains, the quiet stillness seemed to suspend time as if suspecting the dark intentions that now stirred within the heart of the infamous building.

In the cold winter air, the seven cars came to a precise stop, aligning themselves with the other vehicles in a calculated formation. The sound of car doors opening broke the silence, and figures clad in long black leather overcoats emerged, emanating an air of calculated intent. Two individuals stationed themselves near the lead Mercedes, taking on the role of vigilant protectors for their mysterious passenger.

With a keen sense of awareness, the occupants of the other vehicles spread out, each wearing dark trench coats that seemed to blend seamlessly with the shadowy surroundings. Their watchful eyes scanned the area, ever cautious to ensure no prying eyes could observe their clandestine activities.

The moon's silvery glow bathed the scene as these enigmatic figures moved with synchronized precision, like chess pieces in a game of strategic intrigue. It was evident they were well-trained and disciplined, their every move calculated to maintain the secrecy and security of their mission.

Half the group moved forward as the area was meticulously secured, advancing toward the waiting elevator with resolute determination. They formed a disciplined line along the walkway, anticipation and allegiance etched into their stances. Their leader's imminent arrival stirred a palpable sense of reverence among them.

Then, on cue, the rear door of the lead Mercedes swung open, revealing a figure whose appearance bore an uncanny resemblance to history's infamous dictator—Adolf Hitler. Dressed in a black trench coat with the collar turned up to shield himself from the biting cold, he emerged, exuding an aura of authority and charisma that seemed to transcend time itself.

Though the sight of this man was perplexing and even unnerving, the followers before him showed no signs of doubt. Their unwavering loyalty painted a chilling picture, as if history had somehow folded in on itself, forging a path for the past to intermingle with the present. They quickly slammed the heels of their black boots together in unison, hailing the man with "Heil Hitler," and giving the infamous salute.

Their actions evoked memories of a bygone era, a time marked by unspeakable atrocities and the darkest chapters of human history. The very air crackled with the energy of the past, an intangible force that seemed to defy the boundaries of time itself.

In that haunting moment, the mountain seemed to hold its breath as if the very earth could sense the gravity of this encounter. Thunder and lightning echoed through the many canyons surrounding the site as if heralding the arrival of the special guest. The snow-capped peaks bore witness to the surreal scene unfolding before them, a convergence of past and present that sent shivers down the spines of those who bore witness.

The weight of the past and the threatening portent of the present intermingled within the confines of the Eagle's Nest, casting an unsettling pall over the mountain retreat. As the night wore on, the group's allegiance to their leader remained steadfast, carrying an air of inevitability—a resurgence of dark ideologies that defied the passage of time.

Most attendees, male and female alike, donned the infamous black SS uniforms adorned with the black forearm patch bearing the swastika. Nazi party flags adorned the walls, serving as a stark reminder of the dark history embedded in this place.

Amid the imposing backdrop, servants also dressed in SS uniforms but embellished by waiter attire busily prepared an extravagant feast for the group, accompanied by an endless supply of champagne. The air was heavy with a sense of foreboding, as if time had frozen, allowing the past to breathe once more in this haunting setting.

Amid it all stood the Adolf Hitler look-alike, attired in a tan jacket and dark pants complete with the black arm sleeve bearing the swastika. Every person present knew the truth—that this man was an exact clone of their former Führer, sharing the same DNA that had once driven the course of history.

As they gathered around, the resemblance to their past leader was uncanny, unsettling those who saw him up close. The weight of the moment seemed almost unbearable as the boundaries of time blurred, and the specter of the past merged with the present. The banquet hall exuded a palpable tension—a sense that this night marked a pivotal moment in their clandestine mission. The echoes of the past reverberated within the very walls of the Eagle's Nest as if history's chapters were being rewritten before their eyes.

The world outside remained oblivious to the dark resurgence within the heart of the mountain, where the Eagle's Nest stood as a witness to history's eerie twists and turns.

TWO

Three days before Christmas, Jeannie found herself with a short shopping list, determined to get the perfect gifts for her boss, SAC (Special Agent in Charge) Lomax, and her secretary, Stephanie. Most importantly, she wanted to choose a special stocking stuffer for her best friend and co-worker Ismail Flores and his family, who had 'adopted' Jeannie as one of them. The thought of surprising them with her life-changing revelation on Christmas Day warmed her heart.

As she navigated through the festive crowds, the spirit of the season engulfed her, filling her with excitement and anticipation. Each gift she selected held a personal touch, a reflection of her deep appreciation for those who had become her second family in the challenging world of law enforcement.

She resisted each year from simply purchasing gift cards and giving them as presents to friends and family. She had been taught by her stepparents to really put some thought into each purchase. Each present should come from the heart.

She carefully chose a leather-bound notebook for SAC Lomax, knowing he preferred the traditional feel of pen and paper over digital devices. Stephanie would receive a delicate silver locket, symbolizing their shared trust and friendship, besides being co-workers.

However, the gift that carried the most weight was the one for Ismail's family. She wanted to make this Christmas unforgettable for them, and her heart swelled with joy at the thought of revealing her newfound wealth and the possibilities it would bring to their lives.

As Jeannie carefully selected and wrapped each gift for Ismail, his wife, and their children, an overwhelming sense of excitement washed over her. But it wasn't just about the gifts; it was the special card she had prepared to be placed on the tree, waiting for Ismail and his wife to read after unwrapping all the other presents. The thought of their reactions on Christmas Day filled her with a delightful blend of nerves and joy.

This Christmas held a profound significance, surpassing the usual exchange of material things. It was a celebration of the bonds she had formed, the family she had discovered, and the newfound prosperity she could now share with her loved ones. This year, she was ready to unveil a recent revelation that had transformed her life. She had been raised by stepparents, and upon her biological mother's passing, she inherited a substantial fortune, making her a multi-millionaire.

In a world where the true meaning of Christmas often gets lost amid materialism, Jeannie's story reminded everyone of the importance of love, connection, and the unexpected blessings life could bring.

As she drove home, she stopped at her favorite Subway sandwich shop around the corner from her house and picked up a roast beef sandwich, chips, and a drink. Jeannie couldn't help but smile at the thought of the forthcoming revelation. The warmth of the season, combined with the love and friendship she had in her life, made this Christmas feel like the most magical one yet. And she couldn't wait to make it even more special by gifting the truth that would change everything for Ismail's family and bring them all even closer together.

Jeannie's final stop before arriving home was to pick up a pumpkin pie for her chatty yet completely reliable next-door neighbors, Delores and her husband, Walter. The neighborhood's unofficial watchdogs, nothing escaped Delores' keen observation. Both Delores and Walter had obtained concealed weapon permits, which never failed to amuse Jeannie as she imagined them going about their daily routines armed.

Despite Delores' inquisitiveness, Jeannie considered herself blessed to have such wonderful neighbors. They had become like family, always looking out for her home and caring for her beloved koi in the aquarium and the outdoor pond whenever she was away. Their kindness even extended to taking care of her after she had been wounded in a recent shootout, a gesture that touched Jeannie deeply.

Admittedly, Delores' nosiness could sometimes be a bit overwhelming, as she wanted to know every detail of Jeannie's life. Her firm rule over the homeowners' association (HOA) also often led to humorous neighborhood tales. But underneath it all, there was a genuine bond between Jeannie and her neighbors, a connection she cherished.

As she carried the pumpkin pie home, Jeannie couldn't help but smile at the thought of sharing it with Delores and Walter. In her heart, they were more than just neighbors; they were pillars of support, friendship, and community. They had each other's backs, and their presence made the neighborhood feel like a warm and welcoming place to call home.

Jeannie felt an overwhelming sense of gratitude for the people in her life. From her supportive co-workers and best friend Ismail to her reliable neighbors Delores and Walter, each relationship brought a unique joy and meaning. And in the spirit of Christmas, she couldn't wait to share her good news with them all, knowing the bonds they shared would only grow stronger with this newfound abundance in her life.

EAGLE'S NEST

Lt. Detwrick stood with unwavering resolve before the assembled group of SS officers in the Eagle's Nest. He commanded attention with a deliberate tap on his glass of champagne, bringing the conversations among the attendees to an abrupt halt. "Ladies and gentlemen," he began, his voice resonating with authority. He clicked his boots together, a gesture of discipline and respect. "May I present our Führer, Adolf Hitler. Heil Hitler."

The room erupted with the resounding chant of "Heil Hitler" three times, the echoes of the past reverberating through the hearts of those present. The Hitler clone, the living embodiment of their shared legacy, acknowledged the salute with a slight raise of his right hand, a gesture of gratitude that spoke volumes.

With a commanding presence, the clone folded his arms across his chest, his piercing gaze sweeping across the room, seeking to establish eye contact with every officer. "Today, the Fourth Reich is reborn," he declared, his voice carrying an air of determination that sent shivers down their spines.

He paused, allowing the impact of his words to sink in, before continuing, "My father once dreamed of a world forged by Aryan blood—a vision that was betrayed by traitorous generals. Let me make this clear: I shall not repeat his mistakes. Our resolve will not waver, nor will we falter in our mission." He waited for the applause to die down before continuing.

"If men wish to live, they are forced to kill others. The entire struggle for survival is a conquest of the means of existence, which, in turn, eliminates others from these same sources of subsistence. As long as there are peoples on this earth, there will be nations against nations, and they will be forced to protect their vital rights in the same way as the individual is forced to protect his rights. One is either the hammer or the anvil.

"We confess it is our purpose to once again prepare the German people for the role of the hammer. We admit freely and openly that if our movement is victorious, and this time it will be, we will be concerned day and night with the question of how to produce the armed forces that foreign governments have limited in size. We solemnly confess that we consider everyone a scoundrel who does not try day and night to figure out a way to violate this restriction. We will take every step that strengthens our arms, augments the number of our forces, and increases the strength of our people. We confess further that we will dash anyone to pieces who should dare hinder us in this undertaking.

"Our rights will be protected only when the German Reich, the Fourth Reich, is again supported by the point of the German dagger." More applause broke out.

"Nothing is possible unless one will commands, one will that must be obeyed by others, beginning at the top and ending only at the very bottom. This is the expression of an authoritarian state – not of a weak, babbling democracy – where everyone is proud to obey. I will, likewise, be obeyed when I take command."

With a steely determination, the clone laid bare his vision for the Fourth Reich, a vision that echoed the dark ideologies of the past. "The world has grown weak," he proclaimed, his words fueled by a fanatical conviction. "It is now tainted not only by Jews but also by other races that should not be allowed to coexist with our new order." The crowd continued to feed off his every word, and his energy grew with every sentence.

"First, we will secure my rise to power. The Organization will use manipulation, propaganda, and ruthless tactics to garner support and followers around the world. We shall dissolve the Fatherland's existing government, following in my father's footsteps. We will dismantle their parliamentary and federal democracy and assert the establishment of a strong leadership firmly rooted in a singular vision.

"Second, we will begin my expansionist policies for aggressive territorial attainment, seeking to dominate not only the Fatherland's neighboring countries but also countries around the world, imposing our ideology on them.

"Third, embracing my father's ideology, we will promote Aryan racial supremacy and seek to marginalize and persecute minority groups, particularly targeting Jews, homosexuals, and other undesirables. When I feel it is right, we will pursue policies of genocide and ethnic cleansing, and this time, we will not be stopped." More deafening "Heil Hitler" shouts caused the Hitler clone to pause.

"Now, we will meet resistance. We will suppress any opposition with strategic acts of terrorism and assassinations, leading to a climate of fear, censorship, and totalitarian control over media, education, and public discourse." More cheer rained from the crowd. A few women were in tears.

"My comrades, history has taught us harsh lessons. My progenitor made a grievous error, placing trust in those he believed to be loyal. Alas, Goering, Himmler, and others revealed their treacherous hearts," he thundered, his voice resounding through the hall. "Hear me well, for this is a dire warning: Your allegiance to me must be unwavering and prompt. Your every move will be scrutinized, and, should the need arise, you might be called upon to undergo a test of truth, a polygraph. Any slightest flicker of disloyalty shall be met with an unyielding fate." He paused, his eyes sweeping across the assembled gathering, noting some succumbing to trepidation.

"Once the Fourth Reich establishes an unyielding grip on power, the time shall come to unfurl the grand design of our military might, launching forth to conquer nations under the banner of our ideology. A resolute program of military expansion and unwavering aggression will enforce my vision upon the world, sparing no thought for the toll of war or human anguish. The shadows of defeat will never taint our path again," he proclaimed, pausing briefly to quench his thirst with a sip of bottled water before continuing.

"The immediate imperative lies in harnessing the potential of Artificial Intelligence. With this powerful tool at our disposal, we can effectively indoctrinate the youth and manipulate them to rise against our adversaries. Just envision the possibilities had my father wielded this technology under the guidance of Dr. Goebbels," he mused, knowing no response was necessary.

"Tomorrow marks the commencement of our initial assault on the vulnerable world, utilizing AI to its fullest extent under Lt. Detwrick's command. As our supporters multiply, be prepared to execute precise assassinations on targets I shall designate. These strategic eliminations of political figures will pave the way for our infiltration into political systems worldwide, securing power and control over nations, sowing unrest, and propagating our ideologies to spread chaos within societies."

"My father's use of V-2 rockets in the latter stages of his plan to invade Great Britain was an unfortunate missed opportunity, but fear not, for we shall chart a new course. The development of our brilliant plan involves the creation of biological weapons, meticulously engineered to target specific ethnic groups, thus advancing my vision of racial purity and supremacy."

"The terror instilled in the hearts of our enemies and the unwavering loyalty of our followers shall be our strengths. Tonight marks the beginning of a legacy that would make my father proud. Together, we shall resurrect Nazi Germany from the ashes of World War II."

"Heil Hitler! Heil Hitler! Heil Hitler!" the crowd chanted in fervent unison.

As the speech concluded, rather than displaying signs of exhaustion, the clone appeared invigorated. He moved around the room with grace, deftly avoiding any offered food or dessert. He efficiently scheduled future appointments with various individuals, dedicating considerable time to converse with Lt. Detwrick, which some of the generals present seemed to regard with disdain.

As the gathering began to disperse, the Hitler clone finally decided to help himself to some vegetables from the food table and grabbed another bottle of water. Across the room, many people couldn't help but stare at the inspirational leader, amazed at how uncannily he resembled their original Führer.

Among those who paid particular attention to his appearance and mannerisms was Colonel Muller, a protégé of the late Dr. Hausser, whose tragic demise had been orchestrated by Interpol agent Sean Delaney. Both the Führer and Colonel Muller shared clandestine ambitions, conducting secret experiments that delved into the unsettling realm of surrogate mothers and their potential use in their pursuits. Their collaboration in such endeavors remained shrouded in secrecy, away from the crowd's prying eyes.

THREE

As Jeannie arrived at Ismail's home, she couldn't help but be charmed by the festive Christmas decorations adorning the exterior. Seeing her friend's family thriving and growing over the years brought a warm smile to her face. Ismail's wife warmly greeted Jeannie at the front door, where they exchanged heartfelt hugs, a testament to the strong bond they shared. Together, they placed Jeannie's thoughtful presents under the beautifully adorned tree, as Ismail's children rushed over to shower 'Aunt Jeannie' with affectionate hugs.

Their friendship had evolved far beyond that of mere colleagues; Jeannie and Ismail had become like family to each other. Ismail had grown to be a trusted older brother figure for Jeannie, and they had supported one another through thick and thin. The challenges they faced together, including surviving dangerous situations and even gunshot wounds during their investigations, had forged an unbreakable connection between them.

One case had left a profound impact on Ismail. It involved the murder of the niece of a former SS death camp guard, and the intensity of the investigation had taken a significant toll on him. A grave injury during the case left him paralyzed for several weeks, compounding his emotional burden. The weight of the investigation and its impact on his physical health had plunged him into a dark depression, leading him to contemplate despairing thoughts.

However, with Jeannie's unwavering support and the love of his family, Ismail slowly found his way back from the abyss. Their shared experiences and deep understanding of each other's struggles served as pillars of strength during those challenging times. As the holiday season enveloped them in warmth and joy, Jeannie remained grateful for their shared resilient bond, knowing they would always be there for each other, no matter what life threw their way.

As the evening progressed, the playful banter continued, and Ismail's oldest daughter won the coveted prize of riding with Jeannie in her Corvette to attend the 8 p.m. mass. Jeannie couldn't help but feel delighted, as the two shared a close bond resembling an older and younger sister.

But during the Christmas Eve mass, Jeannie found it challenging to concentrate. Her thoughts wandered to cherished memories of her stepmom and stepdad, who used to follow the tradition of attending the midnight mass followed by a light breakfast before retiring early to ensure they had enough rest for the exciting day ahead. Young Jeannie, eager for Santa's visit, used to skip breakfast, hoping he would bring her presents sooner.

As she sat through the gospel and homily, memories of those simpler times tugged at her heart. She missed her loved ones dearly, especially at this time of year. Yet, she also felt a deep gratitude for the family and friends she had in her life now. The strong bonds with Ismail and his family and the warmth they brought into her life made her realize that the spirit of Christmas resided in the love and connection shared between people.

Her mind wandered to the recent revelation that her late biological mother had entrusted her to her aunt, who later became her stepmother, putting their sisterly bond to the test as they aimed to shield themselves from societal criticism and embarrassment stemming from an unplanned pregnancy. Reflecting on how her life might have taken a divergent path had she been raised in the affluent surroundings of Myrtle Beach, South Carolina, Jeannie contemplated her present existence with affection and conviction, cherishing every moment and realizing she wouldn't alter a thing if given the opportunity.

After the mass, Jeannie and Ismail's daughter rode home in the Corvette and chatted happily, sharing stories and laughter. Jeannie couldn't help but feel a sense of joy and fulfillment. The magical feeling of the Christmas season wasn't just about presents or decorations; it was about the moments spent with loved ones, creating cherished memories that would last a lifetime.

Once they'd returned home, Jeannie felt a peaceful contentment settle over her. The holiday season had a special way of bringing people together, reminding them of the true meaning of love and family. And in that moment, surrounded by the warmth of friendship and love, Jeannie knew that she had found her own little Christmas miracle.

As her thoughts meandered, the gentle touch of Ismail's daughter's hand brought her back to the present moment. A smile formed on Jeannie's lips as she looked at the young woman, but she couldn't help but hold back a tear. The realization washed over her that Ismail's daughter, with whom she had formed such a close bond, would be heading off to college the following spring. The bittersweet truth filled her heart with a mix of joy for the girl's bright future and a tinge of sadness for the inevitable change their close relationship would undergo with distance and new experiences.

"See you bright and early, Boss," Ismail said to Jeannie on Christmas Eve night after a light dinner. "Make sure you bring me lots of presents," he added playfully, a smile adorning his face.

"I don't know about that. Your wife told me that you haven't been a very good boy this year," Jeannie replied with a teasing glint in her eyes.

Ismail's wife chimed in, "Oh, yes. I've been keeping an eye on him." Jeannie chuckled, grateful for the warmth and humor filling the room. As she bid them goodnight and left for the night, Jeannie couldn't help but reflect on the meaningful connections in her life, cherishing the friendships that made her heart feel full and grateful for the cherished memories they created together.

"Drive safe," Ismail called out as he watched Jeannie start up her car and leave, then he began shutting down his Christmas yard display. As Jeannie drove home, the anticipation of giving her gift to Ismail and his family filled her heart with joy. She knew they would be surprised and delighted by her thoughtful presents. A Christmas CD played in the background, setting a festive mood for the drive.

FOUR

As Sergeant Weber, a slightly obese German with a buzz cut, switched on the car radio, the weather report revealed Berlin's current temperature was a balmy three degrees Celsius. "Well, at least it's not snowing," he remarked, lighting a cigarette. He glanced over at his car partner, Sergeant Schneider, a man about ten years older than Weber with an athletic build and standing about five inches taller.

Schneider replied in German, "It's almost 2 a.m., and since tomorrow is Christmas, I believe the Chancellor and his family are fast asleep. Let's proceed now so we can get back home and into bed."

Weber lifted his walkie-talkie and directed the team, "Alright, everyone, it's time to start our approach to the residence. We'll handle security at the front. Four guards are on duty, likely dozing off near the security screens at the entrance. Stay put at the rear, and we'll signal you to join once we neutralize them. We must keep things quiet to avoid waking the Chancellor and his family on the second floor. Let's meet at the base of the stairs before advancing further."

Two other men accompanied sergeants Weber and Schneider as they approached the front door. They knew two more men were simultaneously doing the same at the rear of the building. Each team member carried a Ruger Mark IV suppressor weapon.

One of the men with Weber and Schneider held a large box wrapped in Christmas paper strategically positioned in front of him. It was so substantial that anyone monitoring a security camera would only see the enormous box, thus concealing the true intentions of their approach.

As expected, a drowsy guard answered the residence's front door, initially startled by the unexpected doorbell. However, upon seeing the massive gift wrapped in festive Christmas paper, the tension eased among the security personnel. Assigning the task to the junior member of the staff, they sent him to retrieve the package while the rest of the guards proceeded back to their slumber.

"What do you have there?" the guard asked, his curiosity piqued as he saw the large box being carried toward the house. Little did he realize, until it was too late, that the barrel of a gun was partially protruding from the side of the seemingly innocent package. In an instant, two rapid shots rang out. The guard looked down at his once-white shirt, now drenched in his blood. The SS officer who had been carrying the box quickly pushed the wounded guard back into the residence, allowing Sergeant Weber, Sergeant Schneider, and the fourth member to enter.

Inside, the fourth SS member quickly made his way to the side of the house, away from the location of the security detail, and unlocked the rear door. Meanwhile, Weber, Schneider, and the third SS member reached the entrance to the security room. They swiftly neutralized the three remaining guards without hesitation, ensuring their approach remained undetected.

They all listened intently for any signs of alarm or disturbance, but to their relief, they heard nothing. The residence remained undisturbed, allowing them to proceed with their mission cautiously and precisely.

Weber and Schneider initiated their ascent up the stairs, the man who had carried the Christmas gift and the fourth SS soldier following closely behind. Upon reaching the landing outside the Chancellor's bedroom, Schneider assigned the other two men to secure the children, two young girls sleeping in the adjoining room.

With utmost caution, Schneider and Weber opened the Chancellor's bedroom door and stepped inside, their every movement deliberate and hushed to avoid disturbing the sleeping occupants. The Chancellor lay on his side on the left side of the bed next to a nightstand holding several phones, his reading glasses, and a softcover book with a place marker. His wife lay on the opposite side, facing away from her husband

and deep in slumber. The room was dimly lit, and the air hung heavy with the weight of the moment.

Almost simultaneously, the chilling sounds of "zip" "zip" shattered the silence in the room. In cold determination to ensure the Hitler clone's order was carried out without any possibility of the Chancellor being revived, coup de grace shots were delivered to his lifeless body. The dark deed was completed.

Weber retrieved his cell phone and discreetly captured pictures of the Chancellor and his family, fulfilling the Hitler clone's peculiar request. While they had been waiting in the car before the dreadful act, Weber and Schneider rationalized that the clone's unusual demand stemmed from his intense paranoia and deep-seated distrust, reminiscent of his father's experiences during his reign.

Weber entered the security detail's room with a purpose, swiftly removing all copies of the surveillance tapes and then systematically smashing the relevant technology. Once satisfied they had erased any traceable evidence, the group exited through the front door, leaving the large Christmas-wrapped present beside the first executed guard.

"Frohe Weihnachten" (Merry Christmas) Schneider muttered as he gently closed the front door, leaving behind a scene of darkness and deception.

FIVE

Jeannie had a restless night reminiscent of a little girl on the eve of a Disneyland visit, her heart aflutter with anticipation. Christmas morning arrived, and with it, an avalanche of memories from her youth flooded her mind. She recalled working alongside her dad, much like Clark Griswold, as they adorned the house with Christmas lights, illuminating the neighborhood with festive cheer. The recollections continued, bringing bittersweet emotions of opening presents with her first husband, now distant memories of a past that had moved on, leaving spouse number two in the same faded frame.

Jeannie returned home from the Flores' residence late on Christmas Eve and discovered a heartfelt note affixed to her garage door. Delores and Walter had left a sweet message, prompting her to check the front door. There, awaiting her, was the familiar sight she found every year—a beautifully crafted basket filled with love and care.

Inside the basket lay homemade delights: freshly baked banana bread, delectable chocolate fudge adorned with nuts, and various mouthwatering sugar cookies. Each treat had been prepared with the utmost thoughtfulness and affection, warming Jeannie's heart with gratitude. The entire ensemble was wrapped beautifully with a charming bow, adding a touch of festive cheer to the gesture.

Touched by her friends' kindness, Jeannie felt the true spirit of Christmas enveloping her as she examined the gift, appreciating the meaningful bond she shared with Delores and Walter. Jeannie headed off to bed after setting the basket on her kitchen counter.

Early the next morning, Christmas Day, Jeannie got to work preparing her traditional Christmas breakfast, a cherished recipe passed down from her youth. She cooked link sausages, crispy hashbrowns, fluffy scrambled eggs, and slices of toasted bread. A steaming cup of hot coffee and a refreshing glass of orange juice completed her "breakfast of champions."

After breakfast, Jeannie took a moment to tend to her koi, spreading the Christmas cheer to her beloved fish inside the dining room and in the outside pond. With the fish well-fed and happy, she returned to the kitchen and placed the used dishes in the dishwasher.

Realizing she had some time to spare before heading to Ismail's house, Jeannie poured herself a second cup of coffee and decided to explore the contents of the beautifully wrapped basket. Cutting herself a slice of Delores's delectable banana bread, she made herself comfortable on the couch, placing the treats on the coffee table.

As she settled in, she turned on the television with the volume muted. The images on the screen hinted at a tragic event unfolding in Germany. Intrigued and concerned, she quickly found her remote control and turned up the volume to better understand the situation.

"Breaking news from Newsmax: Chancellor Werner Altmeyer and his family were tragically assassinated in their home on Christmas Eve. The devastating incident came to light early this morning when the household staff arrived and discovered their lifeless bodies. As of now, the German police have not released any further details to the press."

"Oh, my God," Jeannie gasped, her voice echoing through the empty house as she instinctively made the sign of the cross. "What kind of a sick twisted asshole would invade someone's home on Christmas Eve and take the lives of an entire family?" She couldn't help but feel a surge of worry and anger.

"I pray the German police are making progress in their investigation, even if they're keeping some leads close to the vest," Jeannie added, her voice hushed this time. She noticed that her koi in the adjacent dining room seemed agitated, likely startled by her outburst. Wanting to reassure them, she walked over and sprinkled some extra food into their aquarium.

As she stood there watching the graceful movements of the fish, she couldn't shake the feeling of sadness and concern about the news she had just heard. The tragic incident in Germany on Christmas Eve weighed heavily on her mind, reminding her of the fragility of life and the need for compassion in an increasingly uncertain world.

In his disguise as Erik Vogel, the Hitler clone had skillfully navigated the intricacies of the German parliament, swiftly ascending to a high parliamentary post. Concealing his true identity behind a carefully crafted facade, he had artfully wielded his influence, maneuvering behind the scenes to manipulate the government to his advantage.

With shrewd political acumen, he had strategically positioned himself, steadily climbing the ranks, until he became the second in line for the Chancellorship. The halls of power resonated with his subtle but calculated moves, all designed to further his dark agenda while remaining undetected by those around him. Much like his father, his enthusiasm mesmerized the crowds.

As he continued to ascend, the shadow of his true past remained veiled, hidden beneath the mask of Erik Vogel, a seemingly unassuming figure with ambitions that reached far beyond the surface. The stage was set for a dangerous and suspenseful tale of deception and intrigue in the heart of the German government.

"My Führer, I mean, Herr Vogel," an excited adjutant said to the clone, "How long must we wait until we remove Chancellor Werner's replacement?"

"If you make that mistake again, it will cost you your life," Herr Vogel calmly corrected the excited adjutant. He allowed his comment to hang in the air. "As for my plan, we must exercise patience. We will allow Chancellor Werner's replacement to take office for at least a week before making our move. By then, circumstances will be ripe, and the next phase of our strategy will unfold. Then, our assassins will strike and remove him from office, ultimately leading to my ascent to the Chancellorship."

The adjutant nodded and started to leave the room. "Sergeant," Vogel said in an authoritative voice, "do not forget what I said. Another slip of the tongue like you did earlier will cost not only your life but also your family's. Do you understand?" The now pale sergeant again nodded. "Now, get me Colonel Muller so I can get out of this mask."

Jeannie donned a vibrant, festive ensemble: a bright red skirt, crisp white blouse, and matching jacket adorned with a sprig of mistletoe pinned to the collar. Satisfied with her appearance, she parked her car and made her way to Ismail's front door. As she approached, Ismail's oldest daughter greeted her warmly, exclaiming, "Merry Christmas," and embracing her with a hug. "Hey, everyone. Aunt Jeannie is here," she announced cheerfully.

Ismail's voice rang out playfully from the depths of the house, "Did she bring me a lot of presents?" Jeanne couldn't help but chuckle and shake her head, a broad smile on her face. Ismail's daughter joined in the amusement as they stepped inside the welcoming home, ready to celebrate the joyous occasion together.

Ismail's wife had prepared a delightful Christmas breakfast spread on the kitchen table, and she greeted Jeannie warmly with a hug and a kiss. "Ismail, will you please say the blessing?"

"Oh, alright," he responded with a smile. "Bless us, O Lord, and these, Thy gifts, which we are about to receive from Thy bounty, through Christ, our Lord. Amen."

"Thank you," his wife said. "Help yourselves, everyone; the Flores's Christmas breakfast buffet is now open."

Teasingly, Ismail quipped, "It's about time. As a highly trained FBI agent, I need my nourishment." He playfully piled his plate high with slices of linguica, crispy fried potatoes, and fluffy scrambled eggs and topped it all off with two decadent pancakes smothered in butter and syrup.

Jeannie couldn't resist joining in the good-natured banter. "Keep eating like that, Ace, and you'll have to have your beautiful wife make your suit pants out of spandex." The room erupted in laughter, and even Ismail joined in on the fun.

As they gathered around the table to enjoy the scrumptious breakfast, the joyous atmosphere was momentarily interrupted by a phone call from SAC Lomax. Jeannie's heart skipped a beat as she noticed his name on her phone screen, and she exchanged a concerned glance with Ismail. "It's Lomax," she murmured, a hint of worry in her voice.

Ismail tried to inject some optimism, saying, "Well, maybe he's calling to wish you Merry Christmas." However, they both knew deep down that the call likely held news that wasn't going to bring holiday cheer.

Jeannie took a deep breath and answered the call, bracing herself for whatever news SAC Lomax had to deliver. The festive atmosphere was momentarily replaced with a sense of tension and uncertainty as the phone call unfolded, leaving them all on edge during what should have been a joyful occasion.

"Merry Christmas," Jeannie greeted SAC Lomax, her apprehension evident in her voice. "This can't be good."

"Merry Christmas to you as well," SAC Lomax replied. "I assume you're spending Christmas with Ismail and his family, as usual?"

"Yes, we were just enjoying Ismail's wife's delicious Christmas breakfast spread," Jeannie confirmed. "Is there something specific you need to discuss, or was this just a Christmas greeting?"

As she waited for SAC Lomax's response, her mind couldn't help but race with various possibilities, hoping that Ismail's optimistic assumption was correct and that it wasn't a call concerning a new case or an urgent matter. The uncertainty of the phone call now tempered the festive mood that had filled the room.

"Sorry, but I have to be a little Ebenezer Scrooge on you. We received an anonymous letter sent via the USPS, not email. The sender wanted to give us a heads-up about the involvement of The Organization in Chancellor Werner and his family's assassination last night. It does not go into detail; however, it recommends we reexamine what we have regarding the Dr. Hausser case and the whole Hitler clone investigation."

"I understand," she replied somberly. "Anonymous letters are never to be taken lightly. It seems we have something crucial to reevaluate regarding the Dr. Hausser case and the entire investigation surrounding the missing Hitler clone." She glanced at Ismail, whose expression mirrored her concern. "We'll treat this with utmost seriousness," Jeannie assured Lomax. "Thank you for the heads-up, even on Christmas morning. We'll get right to it, and I'll keep you updated on any developments."

"No. I want the two of you to celebrate Christmas. This can wait until Monday. I'll get back to you if anything urgent comes up causing me to call you in. Now, tell Ismail to watch how much linguica he is eating; I've noticed some love handles lately."

Jeannie laughed. "Will do, sir, and again, Merry Christmas." As she ended the call, her thoughts shifted to the investigation and the potential implications. The shadow of The Organization loomed once again, casting its ominous presence over the holiday. But, as an FBI agent, Jeannie knew the truth was essential, regardless of the time or season. She turned to Ismail, knowing that their Christmas plans had taken an unexpected turn, but their commitment to truth and justice remained steadfast.

"The boss said to tell you to watch how much linguica you're eating today since he's noticed love handles," Jeannie said with a playful grin, relaying SAC Lomax's message to Ismail. The room erupted in laughter, momentarily lightening the weight of the serious news they had just received.

Jeannie started to help Ismail's wife clear the kitchen table and move dishes to the sink. "Jeannie. I know you need to relay the information from Lomax to Ismail. Go ahead and do that now. The kids and I can clean up here. We'll join you in the living room and open presents."

"Are you sure?" Jeannie asked. His wife nodded. As Jeannie and Ismail made their way to his home office, she prepared herself to relay the information from SAC Lomax. Taking a deep breath, she shared the details of the anonymous letter that had been received through snail mail, indicating The Organization's involvement in the German Chancellor and his family's assassination. She emphasized that SAC Lomax wanted them to prioritize enjoying the holiday and not delve into the investigation until Monday.

Listening intently, Ismail nodded thoughtfully. "Alright, we'll follow Lomax's advice and put the investigation on hold until Monday," he replied. "We can enjoy Christmas with the fam and take some time to recharge. Come Monday, we'll be ready to tackle the Dr. Hausser case with fresh eyes. I always wondered if Interpol ever tracked down the missing clone. Guess we will find out Monday."

Jeannie appreciated Ismail's level-headed approach, knowing he was committed to the investigation but also understood the importance of family and the spirit of Christmas. They returned to the living room, where the joyful laughter of the children filled the air as they excitedly gathered around the Christmas tree, ready to open their presents.

SIX

In an abandoned rock quarry at 2:30 a.m. Christmas morning, two SUVs, a Dodge Ram, and a Ford F150 were parked facing the entrance to the site. Minimal small talk took place between the vehicle occupants. All were white males, some heavy, some thin. Most showed off tattoos of Nazi swastikas, while others displayed their biceps. All were heavily armed with automatics and semi-automatics.

Soon, a black Range Rover and a black four-door Chevrolet Silverado entered the parking area. The clone, in disguise, was the last to exit from the Range Rover. The men protecting him were dressed in black SS uniforms with the Nazi swastika armband, all exuding an air of seriousness and determination.

"Gentlemen, I appreciate your presence here this morning and value the opportunity to share my message with you," Erik Vogel asserted, making sure to establish eye contact with everyone present. "The primary objective of this gathering is to extend an invitation to your esteemed groups to become part of The Organization."

"What fucking organization?" the thinnest person from the Ford F150 asked. Vogel did not answer but instead turned to one of his men, who quickly removed a handgun and shot the individual directly in the head. Vogel's other men pointed their guns at the rest of the group, who remained motionless, more out of surprise than terror.

"Gentlemen, please understand that I do not intend to stand here and have my men eliminate each of you. If I had ordered my men to do so, we would have taken you out when you arrived." He walked towards the largest male in the group with the most Nazi tattoos. "Your tattoos are directly related to The Organization, and we share the same ideology. The Führer, the leader of The Organization, desires an alliance with you and your members to join our international syndicate, where we will provide you with resources you can only imagine."

A cautious yet curious man focused on the weapons held by Vogel's men as he asked, "What exactly is this Organization, and what kind of resources are you talking about?" He visibly relaxed, grateful he had not been shot or met with hostility, crossing his arms to subtly exhibit his resilience and toughness.

Vogel took a moment to consider his words carefully, seemingly deliberate in his response. "The Organization is an international group of individuals who identify as Aryans, tracing their lineage back to former SS officers, who share a common ideology inspired by our former Führer, Adolf Hitler." The other attendees talked quietly among themselves, which Vogel allowed before continuing.

"Each of you here represents a small militia unit, and I acknowledge that you might have your own ranking system in place," Erik Vogel began, addressing the attendees. "However, it is essential to recognize that in comparison to The Organization I lead, your structures may appear somewhat unorganized. Today, I extend an invitation to join us, where you can benefit from our highly efficient and well-structured approach." The attendees looked at each other in turn.

"Be assured, by joining The Organization, a realm of substantial opportunities awaits you. No longer will you be confined to controlling small areas; instead, you'll have the power to govern cities, states, and even entire countries. Our invitation beckons you to become part of a truly world-changing organization, driven by the vision to shape the future and wield global influence."

Vogel sensed that some in the group still struggled to grasp the worldwide scale of his offer, perhaps due to differences in education levels. Nevertheless, he remained determined to persuade them to join The Organization, for with each new Arian member enlisted, his cause grew stronger.

The last gift remained nestled on a branch of the twinkling Christmas tree: a festive card adorned with colorful decorations and containing a heartfelt letter from Jeannie to the Flores family. Ismail's wife was sitting on the side of his recliner next to him as he began reading the letter aloud. It became apparent that it held a life-changing revelation that would demand a thorough explanation. The contents would undoubtedly ignite a joyful uproar in their household once they laid eyes on the enclosed checks.

Within that innocuous-looking card lay the key to Jeannie's inheritance from her long-lost biological mother, a woman she never had the chance to know. The letter would shed light on the profound connection that had remained hidden until now, bridging the gap between Jeannie and the Flores family in an unexpected way.

Jeannie anticipated a mix of emotions, surprise, and joy would ripple across Ismail and his family's faces as the contents became clearer. The enclosed checks would prove to be a generous gesture from Jeannie, a profound act of love and gratitude. The large check was intended to help Ismail and his wife pay off their mortgage, providing them with financial security and a brighter future. Additionally, it carried funds to fully support their children's education, paving the way for their dreams to blossom unhindered.

What is this?" a stunned Ismail uttered, his voice barely above a whisper. His wife stood beside him, mouth wide open, unable to find words to express her astonishment. Their oldest daughter, seated next to Jeannie, seemed to grasp the significance of the moment instantly. She wrapped her arms around Jeannie with a warm and knowing hug that conveyed a heartfelt understanding of what had just taken place.

In that emotional moment, Jeannie knew that her gift had touched their hearts deeply. It was a revelation beyond words, a bridge that connected their lives in an extraordinary way. The long-hidden inheritance from Jeannie's biological mother had now found its way to her newfound family.

As the realization sank in, the room buzzed with excitement and disbelief. Ismail and his wife's expressions transformed from shock to overwhelming gratitude, their hearts filled with appreciation for Jeannie's selfless act. The significance of the generous check meant freedom from the burden of their mortgage, the chance to breathe easy, and envision a future of financial stability.

Their oldest daughter, ever perceptive, understood the magnitude of the moment. She knew her family's dreams were now within reach, as the funds would ensure her and her siblings' education was fully funded, nurturing their aspirations and potential.

The atmosphere was charged with love, warmth, and joy as the Flores family embraced Jeannie, making her an inseparable part of their lives. In this magical moment, the bonds of family grew stronger, and a new chapter in their lives began, forever intertwined by the extraordinary gift of love and generosity.

"What do you mean? What is this?" Jeannie asked, her face composed and unwavering. "I thought you were a highly trained FBI agent." Her words hung in the air, and the room was momentarily hushed. Jeannie's demeanor was calm and collected, seemingly unfazed by the magnitude of what she had conferred on her friends. Her question, directed at Ismail, who had just read the letter, held a hint of mystery, as if she knew more than she was letting on.

Ismail, still taken aback by the revelation in the letter, looked back at Jeannie, trying to comprehend her reaction. His mind raced, questioning what she might be alluding to. Had she known about her inheritance all along? Was there more to the story that she hadn't shared?

For a moment, the weight of his role as an FBI agent seemed to bear down on him. The training that had sharpened his instincts now left him questioning whether he had missed something significant about Jeannie.

Yet even amid the uncertainty, Jeannie's unwavering expression gave nothing away. She held her composure, leaving a subtle air of intrigue surrounding her true intentions and the depths of her knowledge.

"Okay, boss lady. Out with it," Ismail responded, breaking the tension with a hint of humor. The family gathered closer to Jeannie, eager to hear the captivating Christmas story that they knew would be etched into their hearts forever.

Jeannie smiled, appreciating Ismail's light-hearted approach to the situation. Taking a moment to compose herself, she began to share the remarkable journey that had led to this moment—a tale of discovery, love, and a newfound family connection.

As she spoke, her words carried a mix of emotion, recounting her quest to unravel her past and the surprising revelation of her biological mother's inheritance. She explained how she had discovered her true heritage, leading her to the family she never knew she had.

With every detail she revealed, the room was filled with gasps of amazement and tears of joy. Jeannie's story was nothing short of extraordinary, capturing the hearts of each family member present. As she reached the part where she decided to share her inheritance with the Flores family, emotions soared to new heights.

Jeannie explained that she wanted to express her gratitude for the love and warmth they had shown her since the moment they met. She wanted to repay their kindness by providing a gift that would make a significant difference in their lives—the generous check to pay off their mortgage and the funds for their children's education. And her gratitude included all the years she and Ismail had worked as a team, covering each other's backs.

Her words painted a vivid picture of a bond that had transcended bloodlines, proving that family could be forged through love and shared experiences. The room was now filled not just with the excitement of the unexpected windfall but with an overwhelming sense of belonging and unity.

As Jeannie concluded her story, there was a brief silence before the room erupted in cheers and applause. Hugs were shared, tears of joy were wiped away, and the Flores family embraced Jeannie wholeheartedly as one of their own.

It was a Christmas they would never forget—a celebration of love, generosity, and the power of family ties that knew no boundaries. Jeannie had not only brought them financial blessings but had also gifted them the irreplaceable treasure of her presence in their lives, forever entwining their hearts in a bond that time and distance could never break.

With her story concluded and the room still buzzing with emotions, Jeannie looked around at the faces of the Flores family. In a serious tone, she addressed them all, "There's one more thing I'd like to ask of you, my newfound family. I need you all to swear an oath of silence about this inheritance. I don't want cousins I never knew coming out of the woodwork, requesting money from their newfound relative."

Her request was met with understanding nods and solemn expressions. The Flores family recognized the importance of keeping this revelation within the confines of their close-knit circle. They understood that Jeannie's act of kindness and generosity was meant solely for them, a special gift that should not be tainted by external influences.

As each family member pledged their commitment to keep the inheritance confidential, a sense of unity and loyalty filled the room. They knew this was a testament to the bond they had forged with Jeannie, built on trust and love.

With the oath taken, the Flores family felt even closer to Jeannie, bound not only by blood but also by a shared secret that strengthened their connection. From that day on, the memory of that unforgettable Christmas, the mysterious letter, and the incredible gift of love would be treasured, cherished, and safeguarded within their hearts—a memory that would forever remind them of the true meaning of family.

"Well," Ismail's emotionally exhausted wife said while wiping tears from her cheeks, "I think it is time to prepare our Christmas dinner. We will have candied ham and, for Jeannie, turkey, mashed and sweet potatoes, asparagus, baby peas, dressing, hot rolls, and Jeannie brought us two strawberry whipped cream cakes for dessert."

SEVEN

Monday morning arrived, and Jeannie found herself navigating the daily ritual of commuting across the Dumbarton Bridge. Although she yearned for the freedom of flight, she was firmly grounded in the reality of bumper-to-bumper traffic, which was a familiar scene for her.

Jeannie rolled down the windows of her sleek Corvette to try and embrace the situation and welcomed the gentle caress of the saltwater breeze from the nearby bay. As it played with her hair, she knew once she reached the bureau, she would fashion it into a neat ponytail, maintaining her professional appearance.

As Jeannie's mind wandered, she couldn't help but think about the upcoming reinvestigation of the Dr. Hausser Hitler cloning case. The unsolved issues still haunted her despite the years that had passed. Nevertheless, a sense of excitement and determination surged within her, driven by her unyielding passion for solving mysteries and making a difference in the world.

Now in her mid-forties, Jeannie's presence commanded attention wherever she went. Standing 5' 7" with blond hair and blue eyes, she still turned heads when she entered a room. Her years of hard work had paid off, and she had climbed the ranks of the FBI to become the Assistant Special Agent in Charge of the San Francisco Bureau. Her impressive credentials, including a Ph.D. in psychology, complemented her skills as a law enforcement officer, particularly during her tenure at the Behavioral Analysis Unit (BAU). She had contributed significantly to the capture of several serial killers and spearheaded numerous headline-grabbing investigations while working there.

Jeannie had earned a reputation for dedication and competence, but her commitment to her work had taken its toll on her personal life. She had weathered the downfall of two marriages; however, without any children of her own, she had lovingly embraced Ismail Flores' children, forming a deep bond with them.

After sharing one of the best Christmases ever with the Flores family, she now braced herself to confront the ghosts of Dr. Hausser and The Organization once more. She was ready to delve into the depths of the case with the strength of her experience and the unwavering support of her team, determined to find the answers that had eluded her in the past.

As she prepared for the reinvestigation, she knew this case would be more than just another assignment. It was personal, a matter of unfinished business that she couldn't ignore. She vowed to uncover the truth, no matter how elusive it had been, with her analytical mind, determination, and love for her chosen family.

Jeannie cherished these moments on her morning commute despite the traffic woes. The scenic view of the bay and refreshing breeze provided a momentary respite before she dived into the fast-paced world of crime-solving. As she inched closer to her destination, her focus shifted to the tasks at hand.

She began to recollect the intricate details of the Dr. Hausser investigation as her mind raced. The case had consumed her and her team for a considerable time. Her thoughts drifted back to the moment they were first contacted by Interpol agent Sean Delaney. Remembering his name stirred up a mixture of emotions—bittersweet memories of a person she had once fallen in love with yet who had remained an enigma in the end.

Their encounter had been like something out of a spy novel—a whirlwind romance that had ignited quickly and burned passionately. Jeannie had felt a connection with Sean that seemed to defy explanation, drawn to his intelligence and the shared thrill of their work. However, as their relationship deepened, she realized he was a man shrouded in mystery. There were layers to him she couldn't unravel, leaving her to wonder if she ever truly knew him at all.

The case had been challenging and riveting despite the complexities of their personal relationship. Dr.

Hausser's actions had left a trail of destruction and unanswered questions. Jeannie and her team had pursued every lead, but some of the puzzle pieces had eluded them, leaving a lingering sense of unfinished business.

It all began with the unsettling disappearances of several young females who bore a striking resemblance to each other with blonde hair and blue eyes. They seemed to vanish without a trace. As the missing persons reports grew, it became evident that something far more sinister was at play.

Interpol reached out for assistance from Jeannie and her team since some of the victims were abducted within the United States. They suspected this might be the work of an international sex trafficking ring. As the investigation unfolded, a dark and disturbing truth emerged.

Unbeknownst to the world, a clandestine group of modern-day Nazis, known as The Organization, had orchestrated the theft of Adolf Hitler's remains from a secure vault within the FSB in Moscow, Russia, equivalent to the CIA in the United States. Their sinister motive was to extract Hitler's DNA and use it to impregnate the kidnapped women, intending to turn them into surrogate mothers for some heinous experiment.

The mastermind behind these chilling experiments was none other than Dr. Hausser, a descendant of the infamous 'Angel of Death,' Joseph Mengele. Dr.

Hausser was continuing his ancestor's legacy on a remote, hidden island off the coast of South America, conducting gruesome cloning experiments with the stolen DNA, cloning Adolf Hitler in the bodies of the young women, now surrogates.

The stakes became higher than ever as Jeannie and her team delved deeper into the investigation. Their mission was no longer just about finding missing girls but also about stopping an unholy and dangerous scheme to bring unspeakable horrors into the world. Determined to bring justice to the victims and put an end to the vile operation, Jeannie and her team prepared to confront evil on a scale they had never encountered before. The battle against darkness had only just begun, and the young women's fate hung precariously in the balance.

As Jeannie immersed herself in the investigation, she couldn't ignore her growing feelings for Sean Delaney. However, despite her internal struggle, her focus remained steadfast on the case. Little did she know that her dedication to the investigation would lead to her own abduction.

The Organization's sinister members kidnapped Jeannie, transporting her to the secret island where Dr. Hausser conducted his horrifying experiments. There, she came face-to-face with the chilling reality that the doctor had successfully cloned not just one Hitler baby but four. Dr. Hausser and The Organization gave three of the clones to high-ranking SS officers and their families, but unbeknownst to The Organization, he kept one for himself.

Meanwhile, back at headquarters, Delaney and the rest of Jeannie's team were determined to rescue her. They confronted Dr. Hausser in a dramatic showdown, leading to his demise along with the clone. The nurse involved, unwilling to face capture, chose to end her life with a cyanide capsule.

During the intense shootout, Jeannie sustained a wound to her arm, adding physical pain to her emotional turmoil. To make matters worse, the Austrian government unexpectedly pressed charges against Jeannie, causing further distress and confusion. However, somehow, the case against her was mysteriously dismissed, leaving her to wonder about the strange turn of events.

Tragedy struck again while Jeannie was still recovering from the ordeal. While working on a case involving the urban computer terrorist group Black Cell, Delaney died in a devastating explosion. His loss was shattering, and every trace of his existence seemed wiped away. Despite Jeannie's efforts to uncover the truth behind his death, her investigations hit dead ends.

Now, an anonymous email had surfaced, reigniting all the memories and emotions tied to those turbulent times. Jeannie found herself grappling with a flood of emotions around memories of her love for Sean Delaney, the horrors she witnessed on that secret island, and the unanswered questions surrounding his untimely demise. Past scars were reemerging, and Jeannie knew she must confront the ghosts that haunted her to find closure and peace once more.

Focusing back on the task at hand, Jeannie steeled herself to face the reemerged Dr. Hausser case. The memories of Sean and their past would have to take a backseat to her duty as an FBI agent. She knew she needed to be clear-headed and focused to tackle the complexities of the investigation that had haunted her for so long.

EIGHT

Anticipation and memories flooded Sean Delaney's mind as he waited in the outer office. He first encountered Mr. Brown, a mysterious figure who went by an obvious alias, in a hotel bar. Delaney had already made a tough decision that day: he had to distance himself from Jeannie. He knew if they continued, their future together would be marred, and he couldn't bear to hurt her.

Mr. Brown's true affiliation remained elusive. He never disclosed whether he worked for one of the well-known three-letter agencies, like CIA, MI-6, or NSA. Instead, he spoke of an enigmatic organization known as "Special Branch." According to him, this clandestine group operated outside the conventional channels of black ops and off-the-book syndicates.

Special Branch's mission was global strategic problem-solving. While their methods occasionally blurred ethical lines, the countries that enlisted their services sought to build a better world. Delaney once asked if they were linked to the infamous New World Order (NOW), only to discover that Special Branch had taken actions against NOW, demonstrating their autonomy and complex agenda. Their approach to resolving problems involved extreme and decisive measures.

As Delaney delved deeper into Special Branch's secrets, his fascination grew, and he found himself drawn to their cause. Eventually, he made the life-altering choice to join their ranks, which necessitated severing all ties with Interpol, his friends, and, most heartbreakingly, Jeannie. His former life ended dramatically with his entry into Special Branch, culminating in the explosive termination of The Black Cell.

Contrary to reports, Sean Delaney's story was far from over, and his reemergence into the shadows would soon bring a new twist to the world of international intrigue and danger.

"So, Sean, give me an update on The Fourth Reich. I heard you had a setback. By the way, I love your new look," the director said with a nod, observing the bearded, mustached, and ponytailed Delaney sitting across the desk.

"Yes, sir. Although it appears I haven't gained the complete trust of the hierarchy of The Aryan Vanguard, I did manage to gather some crucial information," Delaney replied, leaning forward. "The top leaders of The Aryan Vanguard are scheduled to attend a meeting with a member of The Fourth Reich. Unfortunately, I couldn't obtain the exact location of the meeting. Representatives from other Neo-Nazi groups, including The Iron Eagles, The New Reich Brigade, and the White Wolves will also be present."

The director raised an eyebrow and couldn't help but comment, "Very catchy names these modern-day Nazis have for their clubs. Sorry, go on."

"Yes, it's quite unsettling," Delaney agreed. "It won't be easy to infiltrate their meeting given the security measures. However, I have a plan. I'll assume a cover identity and pose as a disgruntled member of one of the other neo-Nazi groups. It should allow me to get close and gain their trust, making it easier to gather information."

The director listened intently, acknowledging the risks involved. "That's a bold approach, Sean. Just remember, safety first. These extremists are dangerous, so be cautious. How are you going to disguise your strong British accent?"

"I already thought of that. I will be a disgruntled member of the WNP, the White Nationalist Party, which operated in the UK. I will say I'm tired of all the talk and no action that the rest of the group seems to accept. I don't think they have the know-how to verify my story from the time I've spent hanging on the group's periphery."

"Well, again, safety first," the director said, offering Delaney a bottle of water, which he accepted.

"I understand, sir," Delaney replied. "Once inside, I'll be discreet and attempt to learn more about The Fourth Reich's activities, their objectives, and, most significantly, the whereabouts of the missing Hitler clone. That could be the key to dismantling the entire set-up."

The director nodded, appreciating Delaney's dedication. "You've done well so far, Sean. Your experience as a former Interpol agent will serve you in this mission. Stay in close contact, and we'll be ready to assist when needed."

"Thank you, sir. I won't let you down," Delaney said, determination evident in his voice. The director interjected another question as he was preparing to leave.

"Sean, if I recall correctly, you and the FBI, particularly Agent Loomis, were deeply involved in the Dr. Hausser cloning case. It's safe to assume you'll be coordinating with them from the shadows while keeping your cover intact," the director emphasized.

Delaney nodded, his expression resolute. "Yes, sir, that's correct. I'll maintain my covert status, making sure not to draw any attention to my real identity. Agent Loomis believes I'm gone, and it's crucial to keep it that way. Working from the shadows allows me to gather information discreetly and provide support without jeopardizing our mission."

The director gave a reassuring nod. "Excellent. Your unique skills and background make you invaluable in this fight against The Fourth Reich. However, remember to keep us informed of your progress and any potential developments. Coordinating efficiently with the FBI is crucial to our success."

"Understood, sir," Delaney replied. "Communication will be discreet and encrypted to ensure our operations remain secure. Agent Loomis will receive updates through anonymous channels to avoid raising any suspicions."

The director leaned back in his chair, acknowledging the complexities of their operation. "Good. I have full confidence in your abilities, Sean. Just stay vigilant and cautious. The Fourth Reich is a formidable adversary, and we can't afford any missteps."

"Thank you, sir. I won't let you down," Delaney reaffirmed, standing tall and ready for the challenge that lay ahead. Delaney knew the responsibility resting on his shoulders as he left the director's office. He was determined to protect not only the world from The Fourth Reich's sinister plans but also the woman he loved, Agent Jeannie Loomis. Operating in the shadows was the only way to ensure their safety, even if it meant facing the most dangerous of enemies without anyone knowing he was still alive.

A smile immediately spread across Jeannie's face as she stepped into the San Francisco Bureau office and took in the festive decorations. The holiday spirit was alive, and the office was beautifully adorned for Christmas, even though it had passed now. Despite the politically correct pressure from Washington D.C. and the higher-ups advising against displaying

Christmas decorations, SAC Lomax, the Special Agent in Charge, had decided to go against the grain. That was one of the many reasons why Jeannie and her team held their boss in high regard; he didn't let bureaucracy dampen their celebrations.

The office staff was getting ready to take down the Christmas decorations and usher in the upcoming New Year. For Jeannie, the whole New Year's Eve celebration, with its tradition of getting drunk and watching the ball drop in New York City, didn't hold much appeal. Even in her younger days when she was married, both she and her former spouses preferred a quiet night in, indulging in a little too much food, watching a DVD, and heading to bed well before the clock struck midnight, no matter what state they were in. The glitz and glamour of the typical New Year's festivities simply didn't resonate with her.

Jeannie felt a sense of relief as the festive decorations gradually disappeared from the office. For her, the true joy lay in the camaraderie and meaningful work they did as a team throughout the year. She didn't need a grand celebration to mark the turning of the calendar. Instead, she was fulfilled by making a difference in others' lives through her dedication as a Special Agent.

As she settled into her workspace, Jeannie knew it would be a shortened workweek due to the upcoming New Year's celebrations. However, if any solid leads emerged in their ongoing investigation into The

Fourth Reich, she and her team were ready to dedicate themselves throughout the holiday period.

With a renewed sense of determination, Jeannie looked forward to welcoming her team members returning from the Christmas break. She knew they were prepared to work relentlessly to uncover the truth and safeguard the world from the threat of The Fourth Reich, especially if the Adolf Hitler clone was still alive and behind the sinister movement.

SAC Lomax arrived next, extending a belated Merry Christmas greeting to Jeannie. "Jeannie, Merry Christmas," SAC Lomax said with a warm smile.

Carrying a large box of pasties, he motioned for Jeannie to join him in the breakroom. He seemed a bit embarrassed, likely realizing he had forgotten to offer the greeting when he first called her on Christmas Eve regarding the anonymous email concerning The Fourth Reich.

Jeannie, who had been occupied with thoughts about the Fourth Reich, appreciated the gesture nonetheless and began walking to the breakroom. "Thank you. I understand it's a busy time for all of us. The anonymous email will be our number one priority. Can you show me the copy? Maybe Darcy and Burk can work their magic and track down its origin."

SAC Lomax nodded, fully aware of the seriousness of the situation. "Absolutely. It's vital that we leave no stone unturned. We can't afford to drop our guard, especially with The Fourth Reich's threat hanging over us. How do you plan to proceed?" He casually helped himself to a chocolate-glazed donut and poured a cup of coffee as they continued talking.

Jeannie leaned against the counter, considering her next steps. "I'll collaborate with Darcy and Burk to analyze the email for any traceable details. We'll check for IP addresses, encryption patterns, and any potential clues that might lead us back to the sender. Meanwhile, I'll stay alert for any other leads that might surface during our investigations. We also need to review all the reports from the original kidnapping and cloning operation. Can you get me the contact information for our legal attaché office in Argentina? I want to contact them and see if we can get any assistance."

SAC Lomax nodded approvingly, taking a sip of his coffee. "Good plan. Let's mobilize the team and make sure everyone's aware that The Fourth Reich is a top priority. I trust your instincts, Jeannie, and I know we're in capable hands."

"Thank you, sir," Jeannie replied firmly, her determination evident. "We have to put an end to The Fourth Reich's schemes and dismantle The Organization once and for all. Just imagine a world with Adolf Hitler back in power – it terrifies me to the core."

SAC Lomax nodded in agreement as he reached for another donut. Just then, Ismail walked into the breakroom with a cheerful greeting, “Merry Christmas, everyone!” A smile lit up his face when he saw the assortment of donuts. “Oh, donuts! I came at the perfect time.”

“Did you add some more love handles, Flores?” SAC Lomax teased, glancing at Jeannie and playfully nodding in her direction.

Ismail chuckled, unbothered by the remark. “Nah, just keeping it cozy for the winter, boss. Besides, these donuts are worth every bite.”

Jeannie joined in the light-hearted banter, grateful for the team’s camaraderie. “Enjoy them while they last, Ismail. We’ve got some serious work to do, and I might have to recruit you to hit the gym with me soon.”

Ismail grinned, giving a playful salute. “You got it, Boss. I’ll be your workout buddy anytime.” As they shared a moment of laughter and companionship, the seriousness of their mission still hung in the air. The threat of The Fourth Reich was real, and they knew they had to stay vigilant. However, they found strength in each other in that brief respite, knowing that together, they could take on any challenge that came their way.

REICHSPARTEITAGSGELANDE

Nazi party rally grounds
Nuremberg, Germany

NINE

Nobody appeared to notice or show concern about the numerous vehicles that stopped to drop off individuals near Reichsparteitagsgelände. The people subsequently vanished within the former Nazi party rally grounds. Had someone been observant, they might have spotted an individual arriving in the final car bearing an uncanny resemblance to Adolf Hitler.

The Hitler clone assumed his position fifty feet below the former stadium and its grand steps, where the primary tribute to the former Führer once stood. He was in an expansive hall attended by several hundred people and blended into the surroundings in his black uniform akin to many others present, who were also wearing SS attire. The walls were adorned with Nazi flags, and a prominent podium with a colossal red swastika flag towering behind it graced the center stage.

As 'Hitler' drew near, the crowd erupted in synchronized chants of "Heil Hitler" that resonated through the hall. "Heil Hitler," "Heil Hitler." The Hitler clone stood confidently before the podium, arms crossed and savoring the adoration showered upon him. Gradually, the clamor subsided, and silence engulfed the room. He replied with a similar salute.

"I want to thank our engineering unit for the construction of this magnificent underground meeting place. I believe even Albert Speer would have been impressed. I shall ascend to the position of Germany's new Chancellor within the next 24 hours," the proclamation echoed through the room, met with renewed chants of "Heil Hitler."

"Our initial objective has been achieved. We shall infiltrate all social media platforms and commence the indoctrination of our ideology through the power of Artificial Intelligence. Those who dare oppose us will face the consequences. My father bestowed unwavering trust upon Dr. Goebbels, who believed a lie repeatedly spoken would eventually be embraced as truth.

"Today marks the beginning of our resurgence! With our newfound technology and unwavering determination, we will rewrite history and establish our supremacy once more. Together, we will forge a new era for our cause!" The applause erupted but quickly hushed as he called for the crowd to stay quiet until he was through.

"The world may have thought we were defeated, but we have risen from the ashes like a phoenix. Our ideology will spread like wildfire, engulfing minds and hearts. We shall reclaim our rightful place on the global stage!

"Remember, my followers, we are not confined to borders or boundaries. Our vision extends far beyond this nation. We will rally like-minded individuals worldwide to join our ranks and strengthen our movement!

"As we manipulate the digital landscape, we shall control the narrative. Our propaganda will be omnipresent, leaving no space for dissenting voices. Let our words be etched into the minds of the masses, shaping their thoughts and actions!

"To those who underestimate us, let them bear witness to the might of unity. Our collective spirit shall overcome any opposition, for we are driven by an unwavering purpose. Together, we will construct a new world order!

"Our enemies shall tremble before us, for we possess the willpower to crush all resistance. Just as iron sharpens iron, our trials and struggles shall forge us into an unstoppable force!

"We do not aim to conquer only the physical realm but also those of information and knowledge. We shall manipulate the truth with our mastery of technology, leaving the world blind to our true intentions!

"As I have stated before, my father surrounded himself with weaklings who ultimately revealed their true colors by betraying him. I do not refer to his generals but to his so-called inner circle. Hermann Goring, Heinrick Himmler, Joachim von Ribbentrap, Martin Bormann—all traitors to the Reich when their loyalty was needed the most. Only Dr. Joseph Goebbels remained steadfast by my father's side until the bitter end."

Hitler's clone paused, locking eyes with each person in the room. His gaze was intense, exuding authority. "I will not recreate an inner circle in the same manner. Responsibilities will be shared among all of you, and if I even suspect a hint of disloyalty, it will be dealt with swiftly and decisively. I trust that everyone here comprehends the gravity of my words."

The atmosphere in the room grew heavy as his followers acknowledged the clone's unwavering determination and ruthless approach to maintaining loyalty within their ranks.

"Today, we control the Fatherland. Tomorrow, we start controlling the world!"

Delaney roared into the bar's parking lot astride his sleek, soft-tail Harley. Clad in rugged, weathered Levis, a tank top concealed beneath a sleeveless Levi jacket, and a bold red headband, he exuded a distinct air of rebellion. As he strolled confidently through the entrance, the bar revealed itself to be the central hub for The Aryan Vanguard, an organization with a dark and troubling history.

Inside, a colossal Nazi flag loomed menacingly behind the bar, flanked by an SS helmet that bore an eerie resemblance to an authentic relic from the past. The atmosphere was tense, filled with an uncomfortable mix of adrenaline and unease, as

Delaney navigated the room with a sense of purpose, not entirely in harmony with his surroundings.

"Jake, over here!" bellowed Aaron Blankenship, the imposing leader. He commanded a formidable presence at 6' 2" and carrying 80 pounds excess. His Levi jacket was crudely modified, adorned with disturbing swastikas and neo-Nazi slogans. Aaron's dental condition hinted at his neglected health as he poured a beer into an extra glass on the table, sliding it toward Delaney.

"I missed you at The Organization's meeting the other night," Aaron remarked.

"I wasn't invited. And honestly, what the fuck is The Organization?" Delaney replied, his words tinged with defiance.

Aaron's demeanor stiffened, feeling uncomfortable with Delaney's response. "Hey, man, you need to be careful. The leader of the White Wolves was offed last night for saying something like what you just did."

"What? What went down?" Delaney inquired, his curiosity piqued.

"This guy, goes by the name Vogel, showed up with his bodyguards, and they gunned the bastard down for saying what you just said. Boom, just like that. I figured my ass was next."

"Why would they shoot him?" Delaney pressed for more details.

"Listen to this. With his unmistakable German accent, Vogel invited not just our organization but also The White Wolves, The Iron Eagles, and The New Reich Brigade to join their group called The Organization. He boasted that their reach is international and that they can fund our goals. The audacity, man. This Vogel guy is ice-cold," Arron said excitedly.

"So, what happened after he killed the guy?" Delaney probed further.

"What do you think? We all agreed to join The Organization. He handed each of the leaders and one member from The White Wolves, since their leader was dead, a whopping $100,000 to kickstart recruitment efforts. He also provided a cell phone number to arrange for weapons. This son of a bitch and his organization must be loaded with cash."

"Okay, so, now that we're rollin' together, what's the plan?"

"Well, our job's to amp up our ranks. Got a meet-up next week to hash out our moves. I'll need everyone's damn help 'cos I ain't lookin' to let Vogel down. The guy will cap me right on the spot, I kid you not. I wanna see you there too. You got a sharp eye, and I wanna know how you size up that Vogel asshole."

Jeannie gathered her team in the conference room, where a spread of delicious donuts, freshly brewed coffee, and a selection of teas awaited them. She took charge of the meeting and began outlining the agenda as everyone settled in with their chosen refreshments.

"Welcome back, everyone. I hope you all had a wonderful Christmas and Santa was generous," Jeannie warmly greeted her team.

"He was to me," Ismail chimed in, his voice filled with a hint of mischief, eliciting a knowing smile from Jeannie.

"Before we delve into our current situation, let's bring everyone up to speed on the anonymous email we received and how it connects with our past investigation, which some of you might not be familiar with. A few years ago, Ismail and I collaborated with Interpol on a case that initially appeared to involve an international sex trafficking ring. Young women with striking similarities were being abducted, primarily in Eastern Europe and the United States.

"The modus operandi was to drug these women at nightclubs and then transport them to a secret island off the coast of Argentina. A direct descendant of the infamous Angel of Death, Joseph Mengele, conducted something unimaginable there. He impregnated these women with DNA extracted from the remains of Adolf Hitler, stolen from the Russians."

As Jeannie continued, gasps and murmurs filled the room. "Dr. Hausser, the infamous doctor, was the mastermind behind these experiments. He held a high position within a modern-day Nazi group known as The Organization. You can check with Darcy, our IT specialist, who did a deep dive into The Organization's background, and you'll discover it's an international group with far-reaching influence.

Dr. Hausser's experiments were successful, and he managed to create four clones of the late dictator. We later learned that infants born from these experiments were given to high-ranking members of the SS within The Organization. However, The Organization didn't know that Dr. Hausser kept one of the clones for himself."

Agent Sinclair, thoroughly engrossed in Jeannie's presentation, raised her hand with a question. Jeannie acknowledged her with a nod, and Agent Sinclair spoke, "Jeannie, why did Dr. Hausser create four clones? Wasn't one enough? And why did he keep one for himself?"

"Before I continue, I must emphasize that much of what I'm about to say is speculation, given the unfortunate demise of the doctor and his loyal nurse, who took her own life with a cyanide capsule during the shootout. We'll dive deeper into those details later.

"Our belief, as well as Interpol's, was that The Organization intended to wait a few years to assess the clones' development. Essentially, we thought they would observe and evaluate which clone most closely resembled their deceased Führer in terms of physical attributes, speech, and mannerisms."

Jeannie paused for a moment, taking a sip of her coffee before continuing, "We think they planned to select the clone that best embodied those characteristics to assume the role of the new Führer while the other clones would be eliminated."

Her team listened intently, absorbing the seriousness of the situation. Jeannie went on, "Dr. Hausser firmly believed that he alone was the best judge and mentor for the young Hitler, to the extent that he even planned on raising him in Hitler's former hometown."

Ismail interjected with a grin, "Come on, boss. It's only fair you tell them about what happened to you during the investigation."

Jeannie playfully stuck her tongue out at Ismail before recounting her daring experience. "I flew to Europe with Interpol to pursue the investigation, and, early one morning, I found myself kidnapped by none other than The Organization." The room filled with gasps and shocked expressions as the agents processed the revelation that their own supervisor had been a victim of such a dangerous plot.

"I was transported to their secret island and held captive there," Jeannie continued. "While there, I managed to gather critical information. I learned about the existence of three clones and the names of the three SS officers and their families, who were each awarded one. But that wasn't all I discovered. I also stumbled upon the revelation that Dr. Hausser had secretly created a fourth clone."

Jeannie's tone turned more serious as she acknowledged the incredible teamwork that saved her. "With the exceptional help of Darcy and Burk, the team tracked my location and, ultimately, Interpol mounted a daring raid on the island. Unfortunately, The Organization had already abandoned the place, and I had been flown to Austria with Hausser as their escape plan." Another pause for a bite of a donut and a sip of coffee.

"After successfully tracking my cell phone, Interpol executed a precision raid on the house in Austria," Jeannie recounted, her voice unwavering despite reliving the intense moments. "During the confrontation, Dr. Hausser began firing wildly, and I was unfortunate enough to be struck in the arm. Tragically, one of the innocent clones was lying in a bassinet nearby and lost its life in the crossfire."

A somber hush fell over the room as Jeannie's team listened attentively to the harrowing details. Jeannie's gaze then turned toward Darcy and Burk, pride shining in her eyes. "But thanks to Darcy and Burk's exceptional skills and dedication, we brought this dangerous mission to a successful conclusion. Their meticulous work and unwavering support led to Dr. Hausser's demise. He was shot and died on the scene, putting an end to his malevolent schemes."

A wave of appreciation washed over the team, and Jeannie made sure to let Darcy and Burk know how much their efforts meant. The room remained silent, allowing the serious nature of their achievement to sink in before the discussion resumed.

"This week, the SAC contacted me on Christmas Eve with urgent news: we received an anonymous email indicating that The Organization is still very much operational and that they were responsible for the recent assassination of Germany's Chancellor and his family.

"Today, the primary responsibility for the investigation lies with me, Flores, Burk, and Darcy, but we should be prepared for it to potentially expand to unforeseen locations. That's why I want everyone on the same page," Jeannie explained with a determined tone. She glanced at her team, ensuring they grasped how deadly serious the situation was. The room was filled with a sense of seriousness and purpose as they prepared to embark on this high-stakes mission.

TEN

Jeannie dismissed her team, instructing them to return to their respective cases for the time being. After the meeting, she and Ismail took a moment to refill their coffee cups before heading down to the IT room, where Darcy and Burk were hard at work.

As always, Darcy proved to be impressively efficient. She had already organized the bureau's file on the Dr. Hausser investigation and spread it out neatly on a large table. Burk, who everyone knew was Darcy's boyfriend as the "worst-kept secret" in the bureau, stood by her side, listing the known individuals who possessed the clones.

"Regarding the people with the clones," Darcy began flipping through her notes, "Agent Delaney managed to retrieve a thumb drive from Hausser. What's puzzling is there's a reference to another clone, suggesting there might have been five of them. According to the data, an SS Officer named Captain Franke and his wife Gerta were allegedly awarded an infant, but strangely, they were never seen at the Buenos Aires airport."

Ismail, eager to gain a clearer picture of the situation, suggested using the whiteboard to organize the information. "Can we put some names and details on the whiteboard to get a better understanding of what we're up against?" he inquired.

"That's a good idea," Burk agreed, taking the black marker and stepping up to the board. He turned to Darcy, asking her to list the names.

"Sure, Burkee," Darcy replied, then tried to compose herself after the nickname slip-up. "We are certain that three officers were awarded clones before Hausser and everyone else left the island. They are Herr Schneider, Herr Wagner, and Herr Werner. We'll categorize them under the heading 'Clone Owners.' Let's add the possible fourth clone allocated to Captain Franke and the last, though deceased, to Dr. Hausser."

Everyone stood before the whiteboard admiring Burk's organized charting. Darcy continued, "While we're at it, let's add a separate column for Claus Meyer, the head of The Organization, and his second-in-command, Rolf Becker. In a third column, we have the names found on the thumb drive: Major Hossteller, Captain Heilderman, Lieutenant Muller, Sergeant Weber, and Sergeant Schneider."

"Who are they?" Ismail was a bit confused as he wasn't directly involved in the cloning case, and instead, he and Burk were following up on an illegal transportation of poisonous spiders into SFO (San Francisco International Airport).

Instead of directly answering Ismail, Darcy held off until Burk completed the listing. The outline illustrated The Organization's main hierarchy.

Clone owners	The Organization	Staff
1. Herr Schneider – Berlin	Claus Meyer	Major Hossteller
2. Herr Wagner – Berchtesgaden	Rolf Becker	Capt. Heilderman
3. Herr Werner - Obersalzberg		Lt. Muller
4. Captain Franke – possible fourth clone		Sgt. Weber
5. Dr. Hausser – (deceased) fifth clone		Sgt. Schneider

With the listing now complete, Darcy smiled and said, "Great. Now, to answer your question and fill in the blanks, Ismail. From the thumb drive, we know the owners and their last known locations. We have Claus Meyer as the head man with Becker under the headline 'The Organization,' with his second-in-command. As for the staff, thanks to Dr. Hausser's notes, we know the individuals responsible for the kidnappings of the women used as surrogates. Lieutenant Muller and Sergeants Weber and Schneider were the operatives conducting the abductions."

"Alright. Thank you both. Here's what I propose: Ismail and I will head over to the Interpol office to gather additional information related to the case. We need to find out how they handled the same data we now have on the board. Specifically, we must ascertain if they located the clones and what transpired afterward.

Our involvement in the Black Cell case and my conflict with the Austrian government caused us to lose track of the clones' trail. It would also be helpful to know if any information about Captain Franke came to light.

There are numerous unanswered questions, so Burk, I'll have you and Darcy revisit the Buenos Aires airport files and photos to identify any potentially overlooked details. We'll reconvene to share our findings and decide on our next course of action once Ismail and I return from Interpol."

Ismail and Jeannie made their way to the Interpol San Francisco office in Flores' bureau car after briefing SAC Lomax about their intentions to pursue the Dr. Hausser case. This visit generated mixed emotions for Jeannie, as it was the very place where she met Sean Delaney and where their romance had blossomed. Since his passing, the office had undergone changes, with two new directors assuming their roles, leaving her uncertain about the level of support they would encounter there.

"I'm relieved we have a moment to talk privately," Ismail commented. Jeannie expected some playful banter from her partner, but she was taken aback when he genuinely thanked her once more for the financial support she provided to him and his family.

Jeannie replied with a grin, "If you think buttering me up and going all *Hallmark* will get you a raise, you've got another think coming!" She couldn't help but stifle a laugh at the lighthearted exchange. She hit him on the shoulder and got a huge grin in return.

"Seriously, the wifey spent the entire Christmas night in tears of joy. You ladies and your powerful hormones! But what you did for my family—covering our mortgage, financing our children's education—words can't describe the burden you lifted off my shoulders. How could I ever repay you? The answer is simple: I can't. Never in my life could I fully repay your kindness."

"Well, first things first, you can assist me in unraveling this whole Nazi cloning puzzle. Second, you must be careful not to slip up and let others know about my inheritance. And third, I'd love for you and your family to join me in Myrtle Beach before your daughter leaves for university. What do you say? Sound like a plan?"

"Sounds fantastic to me. I'll even cover the cost of your plane ticket," he exclaimed with a hearty laugh. They reached the Interpol building and parked, arriving at their destination after riding up in the elevator.

The office had undergone a rearrangement since their last visit. A new receptionist warmly greeted them and invited them to take a seat. After a brief wait, the new director, Peter Costello, emerged and exchanged handshakes with Ismail and Jeannie before inviting them into his office. Jeannie couldn't help but recall that it used to be Sean Delaney's office.

"It's a pleasure to meet you both. Your reputations precede you. First, the investigation into the Ark of the Covenant, and then, the Nazi cloning case. Impressive work," Director Costello acknowledged. "Agent Loomis, my sincere condolences on your loss; I know you and Sean Delaney were close. His passing was a significant tragedy for our organization."

Jeannie responded, "Thank you, Director Costello. Yes, recalling the Ark of the Covenant case certainly brings back memories. We encountered some unexpected challenges, but we learned a lot from it. Losing Sean was, indeed, a tremendous blow to Interpol. Please, call me Jeannie."

"Jeannie it is. So, what can I do for you and the FBI?" Director Costello inquired.

"We recently received an anonymous email alerting us that The Organization has grown highly active, and they claim responsibility for the Chancellor of Germany's recent assassination," Jeannie explained.

"Which Chancellor?" Costello inquired further.

"I'm sorry?" Jeannie responded, intrigued.

"Earlier today, only thirteen days after Chancellor Werner Altmeyer and his entire family were assassinated, Chancellor Fischer and his fiancé were killed in a car bombing. The new Chancellor, let me check... Ah, yes, his name is Erik Vogel. He's relatively young, but our intelligence indicates he has risen swiftly through the German government's ranks," Costello shared while shuffling through papers on his desk.

Jeannie's sole response was a puzzled "huh" as she processed the fresh information. Ismail interjected into the conversation, addressing the director directly. "Director, after Jeannie's return from the incident in Austria, she and Agent Delaney immediately delved into other investigations, and we never got an update on the progress of the missing clone case."

"Well, that was two directors ago, and honestly, it never came up on my radar. I assumed our offices in Europe were conducting the follow-up, but you know what they say about assuming anything," he admitted with a hint of regret in his voice. Without further delay, he reached for his phone and dialed his secretary.

"Helen, please find the file on the Dr. Hausser cloning investigation and make a copy of its contents. Bring them to my office once it's done. Thank you," he instructed, determined to rectify the situation and locate the missing information.

"Here's my proposal," he said, taking a thoughtful pause. "I'll take a thorough look at the file and send requests to our other offices. Once I gather all the information, I'll get in touch with you, and then we can compare notes."

ELEVEN

WOLF'S LAIR

Four days after Christmas, a caravan of black vehicles, mostly Mercedes, presented an elegant convoy along a winding road, spanning nearly three hours of travel. The land where these vehicles ventured was shrouded in secrecy under the ownership of The Organization. With many locals still immersed in the festive spirit, the passing convoy of cars drew little attention, seemingly en route to the now-closed tourist attraction, Hitler's Wolf's Lair.

Approximately eight kilometers from the quaint East Prussian town of Ketrzyn, nestled within the Masurian woods near the village of Gorlitz in Ostpreuben, this fortified structure once served as Hitler's Eastern Front military headquarters during World War II. Hidden deep within the Polish forest, the lair held a history steeped in infamy.

For 850 days, from 1941 to 1944, the infamous Nazi dictator occupied this complex before eventually retreating to his Berlin bunker. However, it was on July

20, 1944, that the site bore witness to the attempted assassination of Hitler. Claus von Stauffenberg, the Reserve Army Command Chief of Staff, planted a bomb within the structure, attempting to end the dictator's reign of terror. His plan failed.

Like Reichsparteitagsgelände in Nuremberg, Germany, where the Nazi party held their grand rallies, The Organization had covertly constructed a hidden building beneath the original Wolf's Lair. This subterranean structure rivaled the spaciousness of Nuremberg, evoking memories of the past but with distinct differences. The walls were adorned with Nazi flags, yet the updated version of the lair did not embody the stark austerity of the structure from World War II. Instead, it bore a modern, less Spartan appearance, reflecting The Organization's contemporary influence and vision.

A contingent of heavily armed SS personnel clothed in black uniforms stood at rigid attention outside the concealed structure, forming an imposing sight as the procession of vehicles arrived. The gathering numbered well over 200 people, all eagerly waiting for 'Hitler' to appear.

As a vehicle door swung open, the atmosphere instantly transformed. Those in the vicinity snapped to attention, the sharp sound of their highly polished black boots striking together reverberating through the forest. The chant of "Heil Hitler" intermingled with the echoes, rising with fervor as 'Hitler' briskly walked toward the entrance of the new Wolf's Lair. The scene was charged with an unsettling reverence, evoking memories of a dark past as the enigmatic figure made his way into the heart of the concealed stronghold.

As 'Hitler' entered the room, the atmosphere was charged with fervor. Everyone in attendance snapped to attention, their voices uniting in a resounding chorus of "Heil Hitler," accompanied by the familiar salute. They held their arms aloft until 'Hitler' reached the head of the table. In a somewhat comical manner, 'Hitler' playfully returned the salute to those gathered. Then, to inject a moment of levity, he jokingly bent under the table, saying, "I need to check for briefcases." Laughter erupted throughout the room, embracing the moment of camaraderie and shared amusement.

Flanking 'Hitler' on either side stood Claus Meyer, the head of The Organization until 'Hitler' assumed command, and his trusted second in command, Rolf Becker. 'Hitler' exchanged nods with Major Hossteller, Captain Heilderman, Lieutenant Muller, and Sergeants Weber and Schneider on the opposite side of the table. The air in the room was palpable with tense authority, everyone occupying a distinct place in the hierarchy of power.

The clone began, "First, I want to acknowledge Lieutenant Muller and commend the efforts of Sergeants Weber and Schneider in successfully removing one of the last obstacles for my ascent to Chancellor of the Fatherland through the assassination of Werner Altmeyer. I trust necessary measures have been taken to eliminate the final person standing in the way of my rise to power?"

Weber and Schneider turned their attention to Lieutenant Muller, awaiting his response. "My Führer, in two days, Chancellor Fischer will relinquish his position permanently, or should I say, posthumously?" 'Hitler' nodded.

"Very well. Once I take over the Chancellorship, I will initiate a new era of strength and dominance for the Fatherland. Our enemies will tremble at the might of the Fourth Reich, and our vision of a united and powerful Germany will become real. The Organization's influence will expand, and we shall forge unbreakable alliances to ensure our supremacy on the world stage.

"I will restore our glorious heritage, drawing inspiration from the past while embracing modern advancements to propel us toward greatness. The people will rally behind me, for they will witness a leader who understands their aspirations and empowers them to attain unprecedented achievements.

"My rule will be marked by unwavering loyalty, and those who dare to defy or betray us shall face the harshest consequences. As my father envisioned, we shall reshape the world order to suit our ambitions and secure the destiny of our great nation.

"I want a report from each of you concerning the status of the orders I've issued. Claus Meyer, you seem rather quiet. You wouldn't be plotting my assassination to reclaim your position as head of The Organization, would you?" The room fell silent as 'Hitler' fixed his gaze on Meyer, causing sweat to bead on his forehead.

"No, my Führer," Meyer responded hastily, his voice betraying his nerves. "I have no desire to regain that position. It is rightfully held by you and you alone." The intensity of 'Hitler's' gaze hung in the air, leaving some in attendance to speculate on Meyer's fate, unsure of what the future held for him.

"How are you progressing with the plan to disrupt the Americans' championship football game in a few months?" "My Führer, we have developed an exceedingly infectious virus with the assistance of the Chinese. We intend to release it during what they refer to as the halftime show. We have strategically placed the virus throughout the stadium, and since it is indoors, we can ensure maximum dispersion. Our estimates indicate a kill rate of approximately 70% of those in attendance."

'Hitler' paused, his gaze fixed on Meyer. "Wunderbar. I wish we didn't have to rely on the Communist Chinese, but I understand it was necessary for our goals. I've heard rumors about a secret viral laboratory being discovered by the media in a city in California. Let's hope that discovery doesn't disrupt our plan," he said with a calculated tone. The weight of uncertainty lingered in the air as the success of their scheme hung in the balance.

"No, my Führer. The discovery of the laboratory in California, though unfortunate, will not hinder our attack on the Americans. Fortunately, the laboratory was primarily focused on creating various viruses for our future use. Furthermore, we have labs located here in Poland and Ukraine that are working tirelessly at full capacity," Meyer responded reassuringly. The confidence in his voice conveyed their determination to proceed with the sinister plan, undeterred by the recent events.

"Lieutenant Muller, I trust my orders to eliminate the other clones carrying my father's DNA are progressing on schedule," 'Hitler' inquired with an air of authority.

Muller cleared his throat hesitantly before answering, "My Führer, this is somewhat complicated."

The room fell silent, taken aback by 'Hitler's' sudden angry outburst. "What do you mean, complicated? I gave you a direct order. Eliminate the other clones. What is so complicated about that?" His words were rapid and forceful, accompanied by spewing saliva, as if he was consumed by rage. The tension in the room heightened as everyone awaited Muller's response, aware of the severity of the situation.

With beads of sweat now visible on his forehead and under his nose, Muller struggled to regain his composure. "My Führer, we successfully located and eliminated, along with their family members, those entrusted to a Herr Schneider in Berlin, Herr Wagner in Berchtesgaden, and Herr Werner in Obsersalzberg. However, we encountered an unexpected challenge when we discovered that Dr. Hausser also granted a clone to SS Captain Franke and his wife, Gerta."

"I immediately dispatched units to their last known address, but it seems that they vanished during the night several years ago, leaving everything behind. To this day, our intelligence unit has been unable to locate any trace of them," Muller explained with a touch of frustration in his voice. The seriousness of the situation was apparent as they grappled with the uncertainty surrounding the missing clone and the elusive SS Captain and his wife.

'Hitler' ran his fingers through the hair that had fallen over his eyes. "Very well. Put all our resources into tracking down the missing clone. I do not want this to linger any longer than necessary. We will reconvene in two weeks in Nuremberg to review our progress."

"Let the world bear witness to the resurgence of the Reich, an unyielding force that shall stand the test of time," he declared with unwavering determination. "Together, we shall build a legacy that history will remember for eternity. The future of Germany is within our grasp, and with unshakable resolve, we shall seize it and make it our own."

At 'Hitler's' command, everyone leaped to their feet, smashing their boots together in a show of loyalty and fervently shouting 'Heil Hitler.' The room was charged with zealous enthusiasm, driven by their leader's powerful words, determined to bring forth a new era for the Reich.

TWELVE

A radiant morning unfurled its beauty in the lush, vibrant jungle of Bertioga, nestled within the state of Sao Paulo, Brazil. The city's population, hovering around 65,000, gradually faded away as one ventured northward, where dense forests and untamed wilderness dominated the landscape with vast stretches uninhabited. The midafternoon humidity bordered on stifling, yet the early hours embraced a refreshing coolness veiled in a thick mist that lingered from the previous night's rainfall.

The air resounded with the animated chatter of parrots engaging in lively conversations with other denizens of the jungle. Amid this natural splendor, Captain Franke and his wife made a peculiar choice: they settled in this pristine setting to raise their young, who happened to be a clone of Adolf Hitler.

Both Captain Franke and his devoted spouse, Greta, shared a haunting realization that Dr. Hausser and The Organization had no use for five Hitler clones. Inevitably, a ruthless reckoning would befall those deemed expendable. This terrifying prospect left them with no choice but to take drastic measures to safeguard their now grown-up charge.

Firmly resolved to protect him at all costs, they decided to keep him hidden from the world's prying eyes. A secluded sanctuary would become his refuge, shielded from the clutches of The Organization's relentless assassination squads. They knew their self-imposed isolation would be an arduous journey, but their love for this unique soul far outweighed any fears or uncertainties.

Choosing to raise him in concealment meant embracing a life of constant vigilance and anonymity. Captain Franke, with his military background, would employ his strategic skills to secure their hidden haven, while Greta, with her nurturing touch, would provide the emotional anchor that this extraordinary young man would need.

The jungle of Brazil became their ally once again, offering a labyrinth of dense foliage and impenetrable cover. Their dwelling, ingeniously concealed amid the natural beauty, would provide a sanctuary where he could thrive away from the menacing grasp of The Organization.

Days turned into years, and the young man matured under their careful guidance, infused with the values of compassion and empathy that Captain Franke and Greta believed were essential to counterbalance the dark legacy conferred by his genetic origins. Yet, the ever-looming threat of exposure and violence was never far from their minds.

Despite the isolation, their bond flourished, forming a makeshift family amid the wild splendor of the jungle. Their devotion knew no bounds, and their determination to protect him became an unwavering purpose that fueled their existence.

As the years passed, the world beyond their hidden sanctuary grew ever more complex, with shadows of unrest and dangerous ideologies brewing. In their hearts, they yearned for him to someday venture beyond the confines of the jungle, to be part of a world where acceptance and understanding could replace the hatred and fear that once defined his origins.

Little did they know the outside world would soon come knocking, thrusting them into a perilous journey where secrets would be unraveled, alliances would be tested, and the true depth of their love and sacrifice would be revealed.

Through the incorporation of a growth accelerator gene ingeniously infused into Hitler's DNA, Dr. Hausser succeeded in creating a cohort of clones with an accelerated aging process. As a result, most of the clones, if they managed to survive, biologically manifested in their early twenties, presenting the prime of youth and vitality.

Today, with both his adopted parents, Captain Franke and his beloved spouse, Greta, frail and burdened by illness, the Hitler clone confronted a moment of profound reflection. Despite their past loyalty and care for him, he recognized they had fulfilled their roles in his life, and their purpose in The Organization's grand scheme had come to an end.

With a mix of sentimentality and ruthless pragmatism, he resolved to ensure they received their 'just rewards' for their devoted service. As the sun dipped below the horizon, casting a soft glow over the dense jungle, he orchestrated a seemingly heartfelt farewell gathering in their modest dwelling concealed amid the towering trees.

The air was heavy with unspoken tension as he ushered them into a false sense of security, concealing the coldness that lurked beneath his charming facade. The jungle's chorus of wildlife seemed to echo the moment's significance as if bearing witness to a decision that would irrevocably alter the lives of these three intertwined souls.

They peacefully departed this world as their 'son' served them iced tea heavily laced with Fentanyl, their souls departing side by side. With calculated precision, the Hitler clone orchestrated their farewell, ensuring they would meet their end without suffering. He had already dug two graves in a secluded part of the jungle, away from prying eyes, to conceal their final resting places.

The thick underbrush and towering foliage would protect their graves from curious adventurers, allowing them to vanish into the embrace of nature, unnoticed and forgotten by the world they once knew. The clone stood by their graves with the jungle's silence engulfing him and a mix of emotions swirling within him. He had a faint glimmer of remorse for their sacrifice but, ultimately, an unwavering dedication to the cause he had been bred to serve.

With his adopted parents now gone, the Hitler clone stood at a crossroads, contemplating the next steps in his journey. Though he carried the indelible imprint of 'Hitler's' ideology in his very being, the experiences of his upbringing in the jungle left an indelible mark, sowing seeds of doubt and self-awareness.

He spent days in the solitude of the jungle, wrestling with conflicting thoughts, grappling with the echoes of his past and the faint whispers of empathy that he couldn't fully comprehend. The absence of his parents' guiding presence left a void, allowing a glimmer of introspection to seep through the cracks of his indoctrination.

During these contemplative moments, he found himself instinctively modifying his appearance, which symbolized a subtle shift in his identity. The once clean-shaven face now donned a carefully groomed beard and mustache, signifying a move away from the embodiment of Hitler's exact likeness. This change represented a small act of defiance, a declaration of his own personhood, and a reflection of the nuances within his complex nature.

As he ventured beyond the confines of the jungle, he stumbled upon people from various walks of life - individuals with diverse beliefs, cultures, and experiences. Interactions with these people presented him with perspectives he'd never encountered before, tugging at the seams of his ingrained ideology. His encounter with compassionate souls opened the door to the possibility of transformation as he began to question the extent of the path laid out for him by The Organization.

He found himself torn between loyalty to his creators and the undeniable human connections he forged on his journey. The jungle nurtured a sense of survival and adaptability in him, traits that now enabled him to question and reevaluate his purpose in a world far more multifaceted than he once knew.

As he navigated the complexities of his newfound identity, he covertly became a figure of influence, using his charisma to sway people toward the preservation of their own cultures and unity. Instead of pushing the extremist agenda laid out by The Organization, he subtly advocated for a world where differences were acknowledged, and peace was sought through understanding.

This transformation didn't come without struggles and challenges. The shadows of his past haunted him, and The Organization continued to exert its influence, seeking to ensure he remained steadfast in his mission. Yet, in his journey of self-discovery, he found an unlikely ally in an individual who carried the weight of their own history, someone whose story echoed both pain and redemption.

Together, they formed an unexpected alliance, striving to expose The Organization's true intentions and thwart its sinister plans for world domination. As their actions rippled through the world, he began to embrace his new identity, blending the remnants of his past with the hope of a brighter, more inclusive future.

THIRTEEN

Delaney stepped into the biker bar, his presence commanding respect among the members of the Aryan Vanguard. He joined Jake and his fellow comrades at their table without hesitation. "Aaron, we've got some news," he began, his voice low and confident. "Vogel just sent an email; the meeting's been bumped up to tomorrow night. We're expected to come prepared with a list of everything we need to stir up some serious shit for those who stand against us." A wicked grin spread across his face, echoed by the chuckles that erupted from the others in the group.

Delaney's curiosity got the better of him, and he couldn't resist asking, "Did he mention why he moved the meeting?"

Jake's eyes widened with concern, and he leaned in closer, lowering his voice to a hushed tone. "Are you fuckin' out of your mind? Just uttering those words can get you killed. I warned you before, Vogel and The Organization are not to be fucked with. They're dangerous, and we should tread carefully around them. Remember that when we meet with them. In fact, it might be best if I am the only one who speaks."

"Alright, let's get started," an eager Jeannie declared, addressing Ismail, Darcy, and Burk. "I arranged for a pizza delivery around noon so we can have a working lunch."

A playful smile danced across Ismail's face as he chimed in, "Did you make sure to order linguica as one of the toppings?"

Jeannie grinned back, meeting his light-heartedness with a dash of seriousness. "Of course, Ace. I specifically told them we had a big baby here who needed his linguica." Ismail nodded approvingly, satisfied with the pizza selection. As they gathered around the table, Jeannie posed the question, "Who wants to start?"

"Darcy and I did some digging on the Internet last night," Burk began, "and we uncovered some intriguing details about the two former Chancellors of Germany and their successor, Erik Vogel."

"I bet he's feeling the heat right now," Ismail mused, the playfulness fading momentarily. "Two assassinations in less than three weeks can't be sitting well with him. I mean, if I were in his shoes, I'd be paranoid every time I stepped outside."

Jeannie nodded, acknowledging the seriousness of the situation. "We need to be vigilant. Vogel and The Organization won't take kindly to us snooping around, but we can't let fear stop us. There's too much at stake."

As the aroma of pizza filled the room, Darcy and Burk commenced their presentation, sharing the information they had gleaned from their computer search the night before. They delved into the histories of the two former Chancellors of Germany, uncovering tales of political maneuvers and controversies but nothing particularly relevant to their current investigation.

Jeannie's mind began to wander as the team listened attentively, sensing something was amiss; a subtle shroud of mystery lingered just beyond their reach. She couldn't shake the feeling that there had to be more to the story than what they had found so far.

Darcy continued, his voice animated with enthusiasm as he recounted historical events, while Burk supported the narrative with relevant data and images on the screen. Yet, as each piece of information was presented, Jeannie's instincts heightened, and she couldn't help but feel they were missing a crucial link.

At last, they reached the part of their presentation that focused on Erik Vogel, the Chancellors' successor. The room seemed to tense with anticipation as Darcy and Burk began to share what they had discovered.

However, to Jeannie's surprise, the information about Vogel seemed limited and sanitized, as if carefully curated to hide the true depths of his involvement with The Organization. It was as though someone had meticulously scrubbed the digital traces that could have shed light on his connections and activities.

Even Ismail, who had maintained his playful demeanor throughout the presentation, now wore a pensive expression. “This is too clean,” he remarked quietly. “We know there’s more to Vogel than what we see here.”

Jeannie nodded in agreement. “Exactly. It’s almost as if someone has worked hard to erase his darker secrets, leaving only a carefully constructed facade. But why? What is Vogel hiding, and how is he tied to The Organization?”

As they continued to discuss their findings, they realized the mysteries surrounding Vogel were far more profound than they had initially anticipated. Clearly, their adversary was far more cunning and calculating than they had imagined.

The team decided the shroud of mystery surrounding Erik Vogel and his connection to The Organization had grown thicker, but now they would eat some pizza and take a well-deserved break. Their investigation was just beginning, and the stakes were higher than ever before.

FOURTEEN

On Thursday evening, Delaney trailed Jake and the other Aryan Vanguard members astride his Harley. His conversations with Jake had provided him with insights. The previous gathering with Erik Vogel and the Nazis had unfolded within an abandoned rock quarry; however, this time, they had convened within an expansive, derelict warehouse on the city's fringes.

By Delaney's reckoning, the assembly comprised more than 200 individuals, each adorned with an array of Aryan insignia. Amid the backdrop of cigarette smoke, wafting pot fumes, and hushed conversations among comrades, an air of tension seemed to shroud the entire congregation.

"Aaron, come on over," Jake's voice rang out. As Delaney drew nearer, he spotted two stout figures – one with a shaved scalp and the other with a Mohawk – flanking Jake. "Aaron, meet Billy and his brother, Pete. They're from the White Wolves. Billy's heading them now after Vogel took out their previous leader at our initial gathering." Delaney and the pair exchanged nods instead of handshakes.

Before long, the collective gaze of the assembly fixated upon a black SUV as it glided through the service entrance of the warehouse, accompanied by three more vehicles in tow. As the vehicles stopped, occupants emerged, save for those within the central SUV. Draped in the customary black SS attire and adorned with armbands, they fanned out around the vehicle in a disciplined formation. When the door finally swung open, Erik Vogel emerged, sporting a brown jacket over black pants and the familiar swastika-bearing armband. A silent thought coursed through Delaney's mind as he observed, "Were it not for the absence of a Hitler mustache, this man would be an uncanny twin of the deceased dictator."

The crowd hushed as Vogel appeared to be preparing to address the group. One of his men, a very athletic-looking SS officer, shouted, "Heil Hitler." The group snapped to attention and replied with similar chants.

"Ladies and gentlemen of the true Aryan spirit, the embodiment of a resurgent Reich, I stand before you today as a testament to our collective dedication and purpose. The flame that once flickered so brilliantly under the banner of Adolf Hitler shall be rekindled, fueled by our unwavering commitment to a world brought to its knees by our will.

"I acknowledge the sacrifices you have made, the allegiance you have sworn, and the devotion you have shown in joining The Organization. Together, we transcend borders, ideologies, and conventional limitations. Today, we herald a new era, guided by the same indomitable spirit that once guided our forebears.

"From the trunks of these vehicles, a symbol of our mobilization and strength, we now offer tokens of unity to the leaders among you. Leaders of various gangs, sects, and factions, I entrust you with the tools of our trade – weapons forged in the crucible of our purpose. The Organization's promise, my promise, remains true: our well-orchestrated network can provide you with the resources, knowledge, and audacity to sow chaos within your realms.

"But let not our actions be perceived as mere anarchy. No, dear compatriots, it is through calculated disruption that we unveil the vulnerabilities of a society that has grown complacent in its supposed stability. We shall unravel the tapestry of their perceived order, exposing the fragility that lurks beneath.

"And as the shadows of our intentions cast themselves upon the world, a whisper travels through our ranks. An event like no other beckons our attention. A gathering on which the eyes of the world are fixed, unknowing of the tempest we plan to unleash. This year's Super Bowl, an epitome of their false unity, shall become a crucible of our ingenuity. The virus of our creation, born in the distant lands of the East, shall make its presence known, echoing our might.

"I beckon each of you to consider your role in this grand theater of destiny. Let us be the catalysts of change, the harbingers of a new era. The Organization, our Organization, shall engrave its legacy upon the annals of history, not as an obscure footnote but as the architects of a paradigm shift.

"Remember, dear allies, as you leave this gathering, carry with you the certainty that you are part of something unparalleled, something momentous. Let the resonance of our shared purpose guide your steps, and let our endeavors echo through the corridors of time, shaping a world that bends to our command.

"Let us engrave this truth in our minds as well. Those among us who dare to oppose our cause shall find themselves transformed into adversaries. Know that the repercussions will be merciless, not only upon you but upon those dear to you. Heil Hitler!"

After the weapons were distributed, Vogel promptly retreated to the shelter of his vehicle. Ensconced within its confines, he was flanked once again by his vigilant bodyguards. The entourage then departed in the same formation it had arrived, a synchronized exodus that mirrored their earlier entrance.

Jake cast a glance at Delaney, a hint of relief mingling with his thoughts. "Least the bastard didn't take lives this time. Damn prick likes to use those fancy words that tangle my brain. You make heads or tails of 'em?"

Delaney's lips curved into a half-smile. "Most of them," he replied. Inquisitiveness nudged him, a desire to tap into Jake's awareness of the situation.

"And that Super Bowl chatter… got any idea what that was all about?"

"Beats me," Jake scoffed, his tone candid. The shift in conversation led him to another avenue of discussion. "Hey, did you lay eyes on those weapons The Organization dropped on us? Now that's something else, ain't it?"

"Hey, guys, I gotta take my old lady somewhere. Catch you later at the bar." With those words, Delaney swung onto his Harley and sped away, urgency fueling his need to find a quiet spot where he could draft another anonymous letter to the FBI detailing the potential threat looming over this year's Super Bowl.

Jeannie sat alone in the breakroom, her contemplations uninterrupted until SAC Lomax sauntered in. He poured a cup of coffee before settling across from her, observing her astutely. "Seems like your mind's wandering pretty deep. Those Nazi bastards aren't worming their way under your skin, are they?"

Jeannie shook her head, a faint smile playing on her lips. "Nah, it's not that. It's the uncertainty, you know? The enigma shrouding The Organization's intentions. The anonymous email didn't exactly provide us with a breadcrumb trail. Even Darcy and Burk, with all their tech wizardry, traced it through a labyrinth of servers before it reached us. The odds aren't exactly in our favor to find the sender. Slim to none, leaning heavily on the 'none' side.

"Our primary focus centers on the new Chancellor of Germany, Erik Vogel," Jeannie emphasized. "Scrutinizing his history yields a polished statesman, someone who wields manipulation and coercion, or someone who happens to be the luckiest individual perpetually positioned in opportune spots."

"Aren't most politicians?" Lomax chimed in with the rhetorical question that hung in the air. Without waiting for a response, he rose from his seat, refilled his coffee cup, and started to leave the breakroom. "Just make sure to keep me updated," he added as the door clicked shut behind him.

Jeannie was joined by Ismail, Burk, and Darcy. The conversation meandered through the intricacies of their findings, each piece seeming too carefully curated, as though veiled by a shroud of distortion. Shared glances and exchanged remarks revealed their collective unease, hinting at an unspoken consensus that the truth they sought was elusive, concealed beneath layers of scripting or sanitization.

"Well, truth be told, folks, I'm at a crossroads here," Jeannie admitted, her tone laced with a mix of frustration and uncertainty. "We're essentially left with an anonymous email throwing The Organization back into the spotlight, but with no clear direction. As much as we'd like to pry, this Vogel character is tucked away as the new Chancellor of Germany and way out of our jurisdiction. Maybe it's time we consider handing over what we've got to Interpol and calling it a day."

FIFTEEN

Once again, the Hitler clone orchestrated a gathering of The Organization's highest-ranking SS figures at the Wolf's Lair. He remained resolute about wearing his mask, maintaining the shroud of secrecy until safely within the depths of the subterranean complex. There, aided by his associates, he carefully detached the latex mask and set it on his desk. Skillfully rearranging his hair into the iconic style of his progenitor—minus the notorious mustache—he transformed into an uncanny replica, embodying his father's likeness with meticulous precision.

On this occasion, he wore a black uniform reminiscent of the attire worn by the SS. The moment he entered the room, resounding cries of "Heil Hitler" echoed around him. He responded with a half-hearted raising of his right arm, replicating the gesture. In that instant, he detected a faint twitch in his arm, though it swiftly dissipated.

"Ladies and gentlemen, I've convened you once more to provide an update on the advancement of your respective tasks. It is imperative that we adhere to our timeline. We've made considerable strides since my rise to the Chancellorship. We are swiftly approaching a point where we can transition from a Chancellorship to an outright dictatorship.

"Now, Herr Meyer, I turn to you. What is the status of our initial offensive against the Americans?"

"My Führer, Herr Becker and I have successfully concluded negotiations with the Chinese. We now possess an exceedingly potent virus that is projected to result in a 70% mortality rate among those attending the American football event scheduled for February."

"Intriguing," Vogel interjected, his interest evident. He turned his gaze to Becker, waiting for more details.

"My Führer, without delving too deeply into the technicalities, this airborne virus is currently stored within multiple vials, which our team is in the process of discreetly installing within the air conditioning system of the enclosed stadium. Each vial is equipped with a remote control activation mechanism. The virus will be released into the standard airflow of the ventilation units when triggered from an external source."

"Have you anticipated the security sweeps before the game?"

"Yes, but with no explosive material used, their dogs will not pick up any signs. We have also infiltrated their security forces, and many of our personnel are conducting the sweeps of the interior."

"And what are the Chinese estimating in terms of casualties?" Vogel inquired.

"They've indicated a minimum 70% mortality rate for individuals exposed within the affected area.

Furthermore, this figure is projected to increase as those who attended the event come into contact with their families and friends prior to displaying signs of infection."

Vogel's satisfaction was palpable as he nodded in agreement. "I only wish their feeble and vulnerable president was attending. That would undeniably deliver a significant blow to their Washington D.C. establishment."

He shifted his focus to Colonel Muller. "Colonel Muller, how is our genetics program progressing? With Dr. Hausser's development of the growth hormone, my intention is to swiftly bolster our forces with a surge of Aryan-blooded troops."

Before Muller could respond, Vogel turned his attention to the assembled group. "Gentlemen, I beg your pardon. In case you're not aware, Dr. Hausser's innovations not only encompassed the infusion of my father's DNA into my own, but he also introduced a hormone facilitating rapid growth. I envision Colonel Muller carrying forward the exceptional work initiated by Dr. Hausser. He has been entrusted with the oversight of our new and highly advanced Lebensborn program." Vogel's excitement caused him to momentarily pause and express his apologies, permitting Muller to address the gathering.

"My Führer, even though the American FBI and Interpol uncovered Dr. Hausser's hospital on the Argentinian island, their knowledge remains incomplete regarding the numerous other facilities we've discreetly established worldwide. Thanks to the consistent stream of surrogate women provided by Major Hossteller, Captain Heilderman, and Sergeants Weber and Schneider, I take great pride in announcing that we've achieved an impressive count of nearly 100,000 Aryan offspring—males and females.

"Forgive me, my Führer, but I'm curious about our production of females. When I initially authorized Dr. Hausser's endeavors, the focus was on DNA replication..." he paused, realizing the complexity of his statement. How could he reveal, "we were generating your father's DNA to create you."

"I have granted Colonel Muller the authorization to initiate the production of Aryan females in addition to males. As I mentioned earlier, these females will quickly attain reproductive age because of the aging hormone. This addition will further bolster our expanding workforce to be ready for the eventual invasions of other nations."

"That's a brilliant strategy, my Führer," Mayer responded with enthusiasm. "This move has the potential to amplify our workforce twofold, if not triple its size."

Colonel Muller's voice carried a note of assurance as he added, "I dare say it will yield even greater results."

Turning his focus to Lieutenant Detwrick, Vogel continued, "Now, I look to Lieutenant Detwrick, who leads our Artificial Intelligence unit."

"Thank you, my Führer. Our team has already made significant headway in infiltrating the most popular social media platforms. Notably, we've extended our reach to include platforms operated by our Chinese allies without their knowledge. Our efforts in social media indoctrination are primarily focused on the demographic aged between 10 and 45 years.

"Furthermore, we've strategically acquired ownership of a substantial portion of television stations. Simultaneously, we're making inroads into networks that operate on a pay-to-play basis." The room hummed with a sense of calculated progress as each strategy put forth aimed at solidifying the Fourth Reich's presence across various media landscapes.

Jeannie returned home, weariness weighing heavily upon her. It wasn't the excessive workload but the persistent frustration that had taken its toll. SAC Lomax had given the green light to shutter the case concerning The Organization, as every conceivable lead had been pursued, ultimately yielding naught. Still, the case occupied Jeannie's thoughts interleaved between assessments of fledgling agents and the meticulous scrutiny of the department's fiscal plan.

She silently hoped for a swift maneuver as she seamlessly parked her Corvette inside her garage and sealed the door before there was any chance of encountering Delores. Following a visit to the nearby Safeway supermarket, where she collected all the necessities for crafting her stepfather's famed 'wet sandwich,' complete with chips and soda, luck was on her side, and she managed to avoid bumping into her neighbor.

After indulging in a long, steaming shower, she slipped into a pair of comfortable sweatpants, adorning herself with a San Francisco 49ers jersey. Finally at ease, she readied herself for dinner. Preparing her stepfather's favored 'wet sandwich' required an assembly of red onion slices, pepperoncini peppers, Swiss cheese, mayo, Dijon mustard, a touch of mild horseradish sauce, tomato slices, shredded lettuce, roast beef, turkey, and salami. With the ingredients aligned, she thought, "That should suffice." She gently warmed a 12" French roll in the microwave for 20 seconds.

After placing a dishtowel on her living room coffee table, she paused to feed her koi in the aquarium within her dining room and the outdoor pond. Ensuring her pets were content, she returned to the kitchen. Balancing her plate, which held the crafted sandwich and accompanying nacho chips, she fetched a can of Diet Dr. Pepper, contentment filling her evening.

She placed the items on her coffee table and turned on Newsmax, her new favorite conservative television station. Her favorite talking head was on, indicating that he would be hosting a special on the new Chancellor of Germany, Erik Vogel. She quickly found her cell phone and called Ismail, telling him to turn on Newsmax.

The Chancellor of Germany appeared on the screen. The camera was far back, as if to deliberately avoid close-ups. She noticed what looked like part of a goon squad to his side.

"Ladies and gentlemen, esteemed citizens of Germany. Today, as we gather to discuss the course that stretches before our Fatherland, we find ourselves at a pivotal juncture in history. Our collective odyssey has been marked by a tapestry of leaders, each leaving an indelible imprint upon the trajectory of our destiny. In the context of this legacy, it becomes imperative to contemplate the ideals that have forged our nation, recognizing the profound influence they exert over our present and our future.

"Germany's history, a narrative woven with moments of triumph and trial, stands as a testament to the resilience of our people. As we navigate the intricacies of our era, it is our duty to meticulously examine the ideologies that have shaped the current state of our society and to draw parallels with the era of the National Socialist Party. The currents of transformation often cloak themselves beneath the veneer of progress, shrouding their true intentions. Yet, the annals of history bear witness to the peril that arises from ideologies that threaten to undermine the core tenets of unity, equality, and the dignity of the Aryan race.

"In our pursuit of a more luminous tomorrow, we must maintain a vigilant eye, distinguishing between genuine aspirations and the echoes of a bygone era, which I believe should rise again. The wisdom gleaned from our past underscores the significance of rallying behind charismatic leaders and their visions. A nation ensnared by layers of bureaucracy eventually finds its grasp upon its citizens slipping, yielding a regrettable loss of clarity.

"Our Fatherland's vitality resides in its ability to glean wisdom from the pages of history. As we map our journey forward, we must remain steadfast in upholding the principles that fortify our governance, regardless of the ebb and flow of the outside world, which appears to be descending into chaos.

"Let us unite under a shared vision of a revitalized Germany at this critical juncture, a Germany that, out of sheer necessity, must expand its horizons and advocate for its beliefs. United as a resolute Germany, we shall surmount the obstacles that lay before us and crush any who dare to obstruct our path. Let us emerge from this epoch as a testament to our capacity for evolution, triumphing over the shadows of history. I extend my gratitude for your unwavering dedication, your steadfast determination, and your resolute commitment to the ideals that bind us as one."

As the speech ended, the crowd erupted in a deafening roar of approval, their applause resonating in the air. Swiftly, Vogel folded his arms across his chest, his stance exuding a sense of confidence as if drawing energy from the waves of enthusiasm that engulfed him.

SIXTEEN

Jeannie's cell phone sprang to life immediately after Vogel's segment concluded. As anticipated, the caller ID revealed Ismail's name. "What are your thoughts?" he inquired as Jeannie picked up.

"That asshole is undoubtedly the Hitler clone. I'm convinced, no doubt about it. How about you?"

"Well, speaking as a highly trained FBI agent..."

"Yeah, spare me the official talk. What's your gut feeling?"

"Any lingering doubts evaporated as that clown's speech ended and he folded his arms across his chest. You could practically sketch a Hitler mustache on his face, and the resemblance to the Führer would be uncanny."

"Agree. Tomorrow morning, our first stop should be at Interpol to see what they've managed to unearth. But unless we have the jurisdiction to act... well, we might be walking a thin line."

The image of Vogel lingered in Jeannie's mind, an unwelcome guest even as she slept. It clung to her thoughts, persisting as she awoke and made her way to the bureau. The morning drive did little to shake off the unsettling preoccupation that had taken root. Each passing mile seemed to magnify the situation's urgency. As she neared the bureau's entrance, she couldn't help but wonder what the day would bring and whether the clues at Interpol would offer any respite from the enigma that was Erik Vogel.

Just as Jeannie stepped off the elevator onto her designated floor, Darcy practically collided with her. "Jeannie!" Darcy's urgency was palpable, her breath slightly labored. "The SAC just received another one of those anonymous emails. The Organization is plotting an attack on this year's Super Bowl. He's waiting for you in his office."

Jeannie smoothly handed her purse off to her secretary en route to Lomax's office, her mind already racing with the implications of the urgent news. Ismail joined her as she walked, having overheard the conversation in the hallway. They were soon joined by Darcy, who, fueled by curiosity and concern, opted to tag along.

The trio entered the SAC's office, a place that had seen its fair share of high-stakes discussions. Lomax, the Special Agent in Charge, greeted them with a measured expression. Without words, he handed Jeannie a printed copy of the ominous email, the words stark against the white page.

As Jeannie read, Ismail and Darcy positioned themselves on either side of her, their eyes scanning the text in a united search for meaning. With each passing word, a chilling sensation seemed to crawl through the air, wrapping its tendrils around them all. The seriousness of the situation was undeniable, and the weight of their collective thoughts hung heavy in the room.

I recently infiltrated a meeting held by Erik Vogel, the Chancellor of Germany. A congregation of neo-Nazis was also present at this gathering. Before distributing a vast quantity of firearms, Vogel hinted at an event that would seize the attention of the entire world, an event strategically timed with this year's Super Bowl being held in Las Vegas.

He was vague on the details, but my understanding is that members of The Organization are responsible for carrying out his order. The intent is clear: to plunge the world into a state of shock and terror, warning the world about the power of their organization not to forget the bloody loss of life.

More details will be forthcoming as I learn more.

Ismail was the first to flag the word "bloody." The presence of this term within the anonymous email raised a disconcerting question: was it intentionally included to mislead and create confusion, or did it inadvertently reveal the writer's origins as being from the United Kingdom? Jeannie's heart gave an unexpected jolt as her thoughts involuntarily shifted to Sean Delaney, who had a penchant for using the word. Ismail had playfully dubbed him '007' in homage to the legendary secret agent.

"We need to contact Homeland Security, the National Football League security staff, God, Las Vegas P.D.," an animated Darcy blurted out in a rush of concern.

Jeannie's response was measured, her gaze shifting to Lomax. "Not just yet" she cautioned, her words carrying a weight of understanding. "Remember, The Organization's influence spans borders. We've learned that their reach is vast and all-encompassing. It's plausible they've managed to infiltrate these very organizations you've mentioned, Darcy. If we hastily reach out, The Organization may detect our pursuit. They're adept at sensing threats and might swiftly pivot to a new target."

The room held a tense stillness, the intensity of their situation underscoring every word. In a world where shadows held sway, choosing the right course of action was paramount to protecting the investigation and innocent lives hanging in the balance.

With the troubling email brooding in the air, Jeannie and her team convened in the FBI's large briefing room, their collective determination palpable. The situation's urgency was undeniable – an impending threat on a global stage demanded swift and calculated action.

Jeannie's mind raced as she surveyed her team, each member a crucial cog in the complex machinery of investigation. "Alright, everyone, we've got a lot to unravel here," she began, her tone both resolute and measured. "The Super Bowl is just around the corner, and we can't afford to underestimate the reach and power of The Organization."

Ismail's brow furrowed as he chimed in, "We need to gather more intel on Erik Vogel. Who he's connected to, his movements, and any trace of The Organization's involvement. There must be signs if they're planning something on this scale."

Darcy, her determination unwavering, added, "We could also focus on uncovering their financial trails. Funding an operation of this magnitude leaves a digital footprint. If we can trace the money, we might find leads to their collaborators."

Jeannie nodded in agreement. "Both points are crucial. Ismail, work on getting us more information about Vogel's activities, his known associates, and any anomalies. Darcy, dive into the financials – follow the money trail wherever it leads. I'll reach out to some of our international contacts. If The Organization has indeed expanded its reach, partners across the globe might've encountered them."

As the team dispersed to their respective tasks, Jeannie's thoughts returned to the cryptic inclusion of "bloody" in the email. Her mind wandered to Sean Delaney, a man whose presence had been a constant in her life, until he vanished into the shadows. Was it just a coincidence that this term was used, or was there a deeper connection?

Fueled by determination, she decided to reexamine their previous encounters with Delaney. Was there a pattern, a hidden message, or some clue that could unravel the truth behind his disappearance? As she delved into this new avenue of investigation, her heart raced with anticipation.

A new challenge emerged amid the flurry of activities. Searching the Super Bowl site for potential threats was paramount, but they couldn't afford to set off alarms that might alert The Organization to their growing suspicions. Jeannie knew Vogel's web was intricate, extending even to their own ranks – individuals working within the NFL's security staff and inside the confines of the domed stadium.

"Remember," Jeannie cautioned as her team regrouped, "we need eyes on the ground at the Super Bowl site, but we must not alert The Organization. Vogel's already forewarned his own staff, and we can't afford to tip our hand prematurely. Stay low, stay stealthy, and let's gather as much intel as we can without setting off any alarms."

Delaney sat in a dimly lit hotel room nursing a bottle of beer from a six-pack he'd grabbed on his way back from meeting the elusive Mr. Brown, or Smith, or whatever alias he was currently using. He'd just given the man an update about the anonymous email he'd forwarded to the FBI, outlining The Organization's plans to attack during the Super Bowl.

His mind drifted to Jeannie. There was a time when he genuinely believed their lives were aligning, poised for marriage and the prospect of starting a family together. But something shifted during that operation involving the Black Cell, an incident that cast shadows over his emotions and blurred the boundaries of intimacy, especially after an episode with a fellow Interpol agent in Japan.

The guilt wasn't what struck him most from that encounter, it was the realization that his apprehensions about committing to a single woman ran deep. Those doubts played a pivotal role in his decision to join a super-secret government faction of skilled assassins.

Delaney couldn't shake off a growing unease as he contemplated his recent interactions with Mr. Brown. The man's casual demeanor belied an intelligence and cunning that set off alarms in Delaney's mind. There was a lingering suspicion that The Organization's reach might extend far deeper than they had initially feared. He began to piece together the disturbing possibility that the enemy might have infiltrated the very heart of the Super Bowl's security apparatus.

It was a chilling notion – the thought that The Organization could have operatives among the NFL security staff and other personnel at the Super Bowl site. Delaney imagined them hiding in plain sight, weaving their web of deceit and treachery amid the buzz of excitement and anticipation. This realization weighed heavily on him; it meant any inquiries

Jeannie and her team made could potentially tip off the Nazis, jeopardizing their efforts before they gained momentum.

Delaney's mind raced with thoughts of the grim choices ahead as he mulled over these disconcerting scenarios. It seemed like The Organization had orchestrated a masterstroke, leaving them with little room to maneuver. The risk of exposure was great with such a formidable adversary entrenched in the very heart of their target. Jeannie and her team might inadvertently send out signals that could trigger disastrous consequences of The Organization electing a different, less fortified target.

Setting aside these disturbing thoughts, Delaney shifted his focus back to the emails he had sent to the FBI. He reexamined the carefully worded messages, attempting to anticipate Jeannie's approach to the investigation. He knew her well enough to understand that she'd be dissecting every possible angle, probing for hidden motives, and seeking potential weak points in the enemy's armor.

Though Delaney felt a pang of guilt for not being able to directly support Jeannie and her team since he lived in the shadows, he took solace in the hope that his anonymous contributions would act as small ripples of aid. He was left with the solitary task of watching from a distance and offering whatever insights he could muster.

SEVENTEEN

Jeannie surprisingly woke up with renewed energy following another restless night when she couldn't switch off her racing thoughts. She reviewed her plan of action while sipping a hot cup of coffee and nibbling on a piece of toast. Newsmax played on the television in the background, but nothing of significance was being discussed.

Jeannie continued to expand upon her strategy as she read through her notes.

PLAN: OPERATION SILENT RECON

1. **Remote Surveillance:** Deploy advanced surveillance equipment and drones to gather real-time information about the Super Bowl site. Use high-resolution cameras and audio devices to monitor the surroundings, crowds, and potential security weaknesses. This allows the team to remain at a safe distance while still gathering critical data.

2. **Staggered Inquiries:** Have team members pose as ordinary eventgoers, each with a unique area of focus (e.g., concessions, ticketing, entertainment, etc.). This way, they can subtly interact with staff members, strike up casual conversations, and glean information without arousing suspicion.
3. **Backstory Creation:** Develop detailed backstories for each team member to explain their interest in various aspects of the event. This will provide a credible reason for their inquiries and presence. Team members can be positioned as enthusiasts, writers, or vendors, depending on their skills and expertise.
4. **Disguised Recon:** Deploy the concept of 'hiding in plain sight.' Blend team members into the crowd by using disguises, changing hairstyles, and altering clothing styles. This approach minimizes the chances of being recognized and prevents The Organization from connecting them to the investigation.
5. **Counter-Surveillance Measures:** Implement counter-surveillance tactics to detect any potential tailing or monitoring by The Organization. Use signal detectors to identify hidden tracking or eavesdropping devices that might be used to keep tabs on the team's movements.
6. **Distracting Activities:** Stage small-scale incidents or activities away from the team's inves-

tigation areas. This can draw security personnel and Organization members away from critical zones, allowing the team more freedom to observe and collect information.

7. **Subtle Information Gathering:** Engage in conversations with staff members that don't directly relate to security matters. By discussing topics like logistics, facilities, or local attractions, the team can subtly gauge the level of awareness and suspicion surrounding The Organization's plans.
8. **Alternate Routes:** Identify alternative access routes to key areas of interest that bypass the most heavily guarded points. This can help the team navigate the site without arousing suspicion from security checkpoints.
9. **Short-Term Rentals:** Consider renting a temporary office space or apartment overlooking the Super Bowl site. This provides a base of operations where the team can analyze gathered data and coordinate efforts without drawing attention.
10. **Check with SAC:** Need more manpower. Any contacts that can be trusted?

Jeannie felt a renewed sense of purpose as she refined her plan. She recognized the need for precision and caution, understanding that every move they made could impact the outcome of their mission. With her team's skills and determination, she was confident they could execute Operation Silent Recon without alerting The Organization and proceed toward their goal with utmost secrecy.

An illuminating realization dawned on her as she gave the list a final perusal. Swiftly, she penned her concluding reflection:

Item 11: Establish contact with Paul Rizzo, the deputy chief of ATF (Alcohol Tobacco and Firearms).

After completing her task, she grabbed one last cup of coffee, transferring it into a portable container. With her weapon holstered, she made her way towards the garage. As her sports car's engine roared to life and she reversed out of the garage, another thought infiltrated her mind – the memory of who she believed was the love of her life, Sean Delaney.

Although she was aware he had perished in the explosion orchestrated by the enigmatic Black Cell in a disused missile silo in Japan, the enigma shrouding his demise continued to haunt her. The blast had left his body so ravaged it had been subjected to cremation, according to the official report she had received from Interpol. Due to her absence from his listed contacts, she had not been promptly informed.

"Why was the word 'bloody' in the most recent email?" she pondered while navigating the gridlocked traffic, making her way onto the Dumbarton Bridge.

Lieutenant Weber reclined in his chair in his corner office in Berlin, a short distance down the hallway from the Chancellor's chambers and the enigmatic Hitler clone. His fingers danced rhythmically on the keyboard as he meticulously crafted his social media post. Eager to express his viewpoint on the recent transformations within Germany, he yearned to articulate why these changes were imperative. His allegiance to the fresh Chancellor ran deep, and he was steadfast in his determination to sway hearts and minds to his perspective.

"Dear friends, I wish to take a moment to contemplate the recent shifts in our nation's leadership. The winds of change have ushered in a novel Chancellor, bringing with him a fresh trajectory for our country. I understand that skepticism and inquiries might arise, yet we must hark back to history that teaches us the significance of adaptability and advancement.

"The intricacies of our challenges in the contemporary world are multifaceted and in a perpetual state of evolution. The newly anointed Chancellor embodies the indomitable spirit that characterizes our nation, advocating for economic stability, a harmonious Europe, and a resolute Germany capable of making a substantial mark on the global stage.

"Some may posit that our historical past breeds reluctance toward embracing change, and

I empathize with these concerns. Nonetheless, history also demonstrates that clinging to antiquated methodologies can culminate in stagnation. We owe it to ourselves and future generations to forge a society that thrives within the present reality while upholding our fundamental values.

"Let us engage in substantive dialogue regarding our nation's future. It is permissible to question and endeavor to comprehend. In unison, we possess the power to shape a brighter tomorrow. Our focal points should encompass unity, advancement, and the collective aspirations that fill us with pride as Germans. Together, we rise."

He perused his words once more, ensuring he refrained from divulging too much regarding how the gradual resurgence of the Fourth Reich was intricately tied to the enigmatic Hitler clone. "Dispense morsels of information gradually to the populace. Isn't that akin to the strategy employed by Dr. Goebbels?" he mused, querying himself.

EIGHTEEN

"Paul, it's Jeannie Loomis. I trust you've been keeping well?" Jeannie greeted, affording Rizzo a moment to reciprocate.

"Jeannie. How's my favorite FBI agent? How's old Lomax?" Paul's voice exuded a warm familiarity.

"I'm doing well, and the SAC sends his best regards. Have you a moment, and are you situated in a secure, confidential setting?" Jeannie inquired with a note of caution.

"Oh, I'm all for the cloak-and-dagger theatrics. Let me shut my office door. All set, go ahead," the inquisitive Deputy Director of the ATF chuckled.

"What's on your mind?" he inquired his tone curious. Jeannie proceeded to brief him on the two anonymous emails outlining the intricacies of the challenge they faced while investigating the Super Bowl site in Arizona. She emphasized the need to avoid arousing undue attention or inadvertently alerting The Organization.

She went on to provide additional information detailing their involvement in the Phantom Train case that led to the discovery of one of Hitler's gold trains. Alarming as it was, she revealed that two moles from The Organization had successfully embedded themselves within the ranks of the FBI, with one even operating within her very own department.

In response, Rizzo pledged to initiate discreet background checks on any agents he intended to collaborate with Jeannie's team. Furthermore, he assured her he would personally visit to Arizona to lend direct assistance to her investigation.

Jeannie extended an invitation to Lomax to streamline her efforts, encouraging his attendance at her team's briefing scheduled in the central briefing room. To add an enticing touch, she playfully hinted that an array of donuts and assortment of pastries would be laid out for everyone.

"I'll make my way over as swiftly as possible. Gotta beat Flores to the pastries before he swipes all the good ones. I don't get it – that guy's a certified food enthusiast, yet he's somehow immune to packing on the pounds," Lomax jested with a chuckle.

Jeannie's laughter echoed through the conversation. "Oh, don't say that to him. If you do, he'll start boasting that he's a USDA-approved Portuguese stud muffin." Lomax joined in the laughter, emitting such hearty guffaws that a few curious souls ventured out of their offices to discern the source of the merriment.

Lieutenant Weber received a summons from Vogel. Despite being in Germany and secluded within government premises, the Hitler clone maintained his facade by donning the latex mask. As Lieutenant Weber stepped into Vogel's office, he saluted with a crisp "Heil Hitler." Still in disguise, Vogel had donned his customary brown jacket and black pants, except for the red swastika armband that was conspicuously absent from his attire.

"Ah, Weber. Please, have a seat," Vogel beckoned, gesturing to a chair. "I trust you've brought along the outline detailing the forthcoming steps to be executed by The Organization. As you're well aware, our most significant operation is merely a few weeks from its culmination in America."

"Yes, my Führer," Weber responded, his tone respectful. He opened his briefcase and carefully extracted several documents, which he then arranged on Vogel's desk for his perusal.

The Hitler clone cast a fleeting glance at the documents and once more observed an unwelcome tremor that beset his left arm and hand. Swiftly, he endeavored to conceal this involuntary movement. "Weber, my eyes are weary this afternoon. I'd appreciate it if you proceed with your presentation," he urged, masking any sign of unease.

"Yes, my Führer," Weber replied as he prepared to address each topic from copies of his notes.

'We are planning to target key economic hubs, using the power of The Organization to manipulate markets, disrupt trade agreements, and weaken rival nations' economies. This could lead to political instability and fuel anti-government sentiments.

"Our cyberwarfare is advancing rapidly with almost total control of all social media sites, television stations, and streaming services. By leveraging our advanced cyber capabilities, we will orchestrate cyber-attacks on critical infrastructure, financial institutions, and communication networks in various countries. These attacks should sow chaos and create distrust within governments."

"The Fourth Reich has begun to initiate disinformation campaigns, spreading false narratives and sowing discord within democratic societies tied in with our sophisticated propaganda machinery, ultimately eroding public trust in their governments." The Hitler clone continued to nod in agreement with everything Weber was stating.

"As you know, my Führer, we have covertly provided funding, weapons, and resources to extremist groups in various zones, aiming to destabilize regions of strategic importance and create power vacuums ripe for exploitation."

"By influencing energy supplies and distribution, the Chancellor is pushing vulnerable nations to the brink of energy crises, weakening their economies, and forcing them into political dependency.

"We have also established strategic alliances with like-minded authoritarian regimes, allowing the

Fourth Reich to form coalitions that challenge existing global power dynamics and promote our ideology.

"By fomenting proxy conflicts in politically sensitive regions, we are diverting international attention and resources away from tackling our efforts in global expansion."

Vogel raised his hand. "With this in mind, I will continue to work actively in weakening international organizations such as the United Nations, NATO, and other regional alliances, diminishing their ability to respond effectively to global crises of our making." Weber nodded before returning to his notes.

"The Fourth Reich has employed espionage and sabotage operations against governments and industries, crippling their infrastructures and compromising their national security.

"We are now influencing educational curricula and cultural narratives in line with our propaganda agenda in the schools of many nations, including the United States. Not only does this allow us to indoctrinate the youth of the world but also to reshape public perceptions and align them with our vision, ultimately undermining the values and principles of targeted nations.

"And, my Führer, to further illustrate that our plans are working, I would like to read to you a piece from one of the American newspapers. The title of the piece is **Americans are widely pessimistic about the state of democracy in the U.S.** An AP-NORC poll finds only about one in ten U.S. adults give high ratings to the way democracy is working in the United States or how well it represents the interests of most Americans, according to a new poll from The Associated Press-NORC Center for Public Affairs Research.

"Most adults say U.S. laws and policies poorly represent what most Americans want on issues ranging from the economy and government spending to gun policy, immigration, and abortion. The poll shows 53 percent say Congress is doing a bad job of upholding democratic values, compared with just 16 percent who say it's doing a good job.

"The findings illustrate widespread political alienation as a polarized country limps out of the pandemic and into a recovery haunted by inflation and fears of a recession. In interviews, respondents are less worried about the machinery of democracy — voting laws and the tabulation of ballots — and more about the outputs. About half the country — 49 percent — says democracy is not working well in the United States."

Weber's progress report energized Vogel as he unconsciously held his left arm. His eyes gleamed with ominous anticipation. His voice resonated with conviction as he added, "This is good. This is very good. Rest assured, Weber, our preparations are nearing fruition. Soon, the world will bear witness to the overwhelming might of The Organization and the triumphant emergence of the new Fourth Reich."

NINETEEN

The spacious second-floor room at the San Francisco FBI Bureau was already abuzz with activity as the "all-hands-on-deck" briefing got underway. Earlier, Jeannie had met with Lomax, discussing the bullet points she intended to cover with her team of agents. He offered several suggestions to support her in tackling the monumental task ahead.

As the Special Agent in Charge predicted, Ismail wasted no time heading to the refreshments table and helping himself to a pair of pastries and a cup of coffee. After grabbing his treats, he settled into a seat near the head table where Jeannie was arranging her materials.

After connecting her laptop to the sizable screen behind her, Jeannie brought up the initial slide displaying the title "Operation Silent Recon." Ismail grinned slightly, his fingers inadvertently brushing away a remnant of a raspberry pastry from his chin. In response, Jeannie playfully winked at him. When everyone had taken their seats, she began her presentation, the whiteboard behind her showcasing the name she had coined for their investigation: Operation Silent Recon.

Jeannie's voice filled the room with a firm sense of purpose as she delved into the heart of their mission. "Yet another anonymous email has arrived that divulges intelligence about The Organization's intentions—a plot aimed at disrupting this year's Super Bowl, scheduled just a few weeks from today," she began. "We must tread with care in our investigative steps considering The Organization's unsettling ability to infiltrate every government stratum and beyond.

"We must cautiously avoid any actions that might tip them off and push them to alter their target. To that end, I've reached out to ATF Assistant Director Paul Rizzo. He's assembling a handpicked team to join our efforts.

"We'll be gathering in Las Vegas within the next 72 hours. Those I select this afternoon need to be ready to hit the road and remain fully engaged until after the championship game concludes." Jeannie's gaze swept across her team, emphasizing the serious nature of the situation.

With a click of her mouse, the room's attention shifted to the presentation slides behind her. Each point she outlined held a pivotal role in their meticulous strategy.

1. **Remote Surveillance**: "Darcy, Burk," she pointed to each in turn, "I want you to establish

a liaison with the ATF. Utilize as many drones and advanced surveillance tools as necessary to gather real-time information, both inside and outside the Super Bowl venue."

2. **Staggered Inquiries**: "We'll blend in as everyday event-goers, each person focusing on a different area of interest—be it concessions, ticketing, entertainment, or even those seeking tickets. Get NFL jerseys to blend seamlessly with the crowd and initiate casual conversations with staff to subtly gather information."
3. **Backstory Creation**: "Develop comprehensive backstories to account for your interests in various aspects of the event. These will serve as plausible cover stories in case an Organization member raises suspicions."
4. **Disguised Recon**: "The strategy here is to hide in plain sight. Alter your appearance with disguises and changes in hairstyle or clothing. This minimizes the chances of being identified and having links drawn to our investigation."
5. **Counter-Surveillance Measures**: "We're dealing with an incredibly organized and well-funded adversary. Our counterparts in Arizona will assist in deploying counter-surveillance tactics. This will help detect any attempts at tailing or monitoring by The Organization. Signal detectors will aid in identifying hidden tracking or eavesdropping devices."

6. **Counter-Surveillance Measures**: "Those assigned to the Super Bowl site will implement their own counter-surveillance measures. Use signal detectors to sweep for tracking devices or eavesdropping equipment that might compromise your movements."
7. **Distracting Activities**: "We'll create diversions—small-scale incidents or attractions—away from our primary investigation areas. The goal is to divert security personnel and Organization members, granting our team greater freedom to observe, gather information, and explore the stadium."
8. **Subtle Information Gathering**: "Engage in conversations with staff members, focusing on non-security matters. By discussing logistics, facilities, or local attractions, you can gauge the level of awareness and suspicion surrounding The Organization's plans."
9. **Alternate Routes**: "Familiarize yourselves with alternative access routes that bypass heavily guarded points. This will enable the team to navigate discreetly without arousing undue suspicion."
10. **Short-Term Rentals**: "Given the scope of this investigation, the SAC has granted us extensive latitude. I'll secure a temporary office or apartment with a view of the Super Bowl site. This will serve as our operational base, where data

can be analyzed and efforts coordinated without attracting attention." (Slide advance)

11. **Decentralized Communication**: "Our communication methods must be foolproof. Utilize encrypted messaging apps and establish codewords to ensure shared information remains confidential. Darcy and Burk will assist in setting up secure channels." (Slide advance)
12. **Physical Reconnaissance**: "Some of you will be asked to conduct discreet physical reconnaissance of the stadium's layout, entrances, exits, and potential hiding spots prior to the event. This will help us identify strategic positions for observation and potential extraction points." (Slide advance)
13. **Social Media Monitoring**: "Darcy and Burk will keep tabs on social media platforms for suspicious or coded communications that might hint at The Organization's plans. Be vigilant for any patterns or connections that could provide valuable insights." (Slide advance)
14. **Crisis Simulation**: "Unfortunately, we won't have time to prepare for potential contingencies, nor simulate crisis scenarios to test our reactions and coordination. You must all rely on your training." (Slide advance)
15. **Emergency Extraction Plan**: "Between Ismail and I, plus the ATD, we will have a well-thought-out plan for extracting the team in case of an

emergency or if suspicions are aroused. We will identify safe locations, alternate transportation, and communication protocols for such situations and pass that on to you once we are on the ground." (Slide advance)

16. **Code Words and Hand Signals**: "Once we arrive, I will issue everyone a set of codewords and hand signals for discreet communication among team members during live operations. This will help prevent compromising conversations." (Slide advance)
17. **Secure Evidence Handling**: "Finally, if any evidence is collected, ensure it's securely stored, cataloged, and analyzed. Implement protocols to prevent tampering or leaks. However, if explosives or other hazardous items are found, back off and notify me or AFT Assistant Direction Rizzo, who, with his staff, will be using our radios."

A renewed sense of purpose flowed through Jeannie as she continued refining the plan in real time during her presentation. She was keenly aware that precision and caution were paramount—their every move carried weight. She held the unshakable belief that, with her team's expertise and determination, they could execute Operation Silent Recon and advance toward their goal under a shroud of utmost secrecy.

Jeannie handed over the meeting reins to Ismail, Darcy, and Burk, and she and Lomax made their way to the breakroom. "You handled that well," Lomax commented. "I've already reached out to the SAC in Las Vegas. I've also spoken with the NFL Commissioner, someone I trust implicitly."

"I shared our concerns about maintaining a discreet investigation during the game. He's given me confidential assurances and even provided a list of individuals he believes we can rely on within his hierarchy. Also, I'm enlisting some agents with IT expertise to support Darcy and Burk in conducting swift background checks on the list."

Jeannie sighed appreciatively, her throat parched from the intensity of the situation. "Having NFL security personnel involved would be invaluable," she admitted, taking a sip of her soda to relieve her dry voice. "Ever been to a Super Bowl?" Jeannie asked.

A chuckle escaped Lomax's lips before he responded, "No, not really my scene. I'd much rather be at home with my beer, a spread of sandwiches, nachos and cheese, and a generous slice of cake or pie once the game is done. Truth is, I usually don't even turn on the TV until just before kick-off. All the pre-game chatter from talking heads wears thin. And perhaps the best part—no battling the restroom lines. There is no way I would pay $5,596 a ticket, and that's probably in the nose-bleed section."

Jeannie smiled at Lomax's candid response, the exchange providing a brief respite from the seriousness of their impending mission.

"Yeah, I understand. If you remember, I took Ismail to a Super Bowl a few years ago after his cousin got some tickets. His cousin couldn't go. It was quite an experience being there with the crowd and all, but gee, when you need to go to the restroom, it was a joke. I got a kick out of some of the fans who paid thousands of dollars to watch the game, and then all they did was sit there playing on their phones. Unbelievable."

TWENTY

Jeannie and Ismail made their way back to the Interpol office the following morning, where they were scheduled to meet with Director Costello. The director's expression bore a mixture of concern and severity as they entered. "Please, come in. I believe I have news that might pique your interest, though I must warn you, it's quite unsettling," he spoke as the agents were ushered into his office. Taking their seats, they awaited what he had to share.

Director Costello retrieved a thick file from a concealed spot behind his desk, its weight and appearance signifying the significance of its contents. He extracted a set of photographs from within, each captured from a distance. The images showcased three individuals, Chinese virologists, to be precise. Their focus was virus weaponization, a topic that carried sinister implications.

"Allow me to introduce you to these three individuals," Costello began, his tone tinged with urgency behind his British accent. "On the left, we have Dr. Ming Tao. In the middle, Dr. Chao-Xing, and to her right, Dr. Zhi Peng." He paused, his gaze focused on the images he held. " Dr. Chao-Xing is undoubtedly the most formidable of the trio. Our intelligence sources indicate she was the mastermind behind the tragic massacre in a southern province of China, a horrific event that claimed the lives of 4,000 innocent people. She introduced a quick-acting virus with shocking results. The other two operate under her guidance."

He then presented them with another photograph that captured the trio of virologists once more. However, this time, the setting was an open-air coffee shop, and they were accompanied by three Caucasian men. As Director Costello elucidated, "This photograph was taken in Peking. We had only one of these gentlemen's identities confirmed initially." He gestured to the figure carefully adding sugar to his coffee. "His last name is Schneider. We uncovered the identities of the other two individuals through him.

The one leisurely sipping his beverage is Wagner, and the third is Werner. Their lineage is unmistakably German." He paused, his implication clear. "As you might already have deduced, they hold considerably influential positions within The Organization."

As Director Costello continued to share the unsettling information, Jeannie's mind raced, connecting the dots between the virologists, the mysterious Germans, and the terrible plans that seemed to be taking shape. A pattern emerged that couldn't be ignored as the images of the virologists and Germans played out in her mind.

The presence of these masters in the dark art of virus manipulation alongside the enigmatic Germans at a crucial time wasn't a coincidence. The pieces were woven together with intent, forming a tapestry of malevolent design.

Jeannie's eyes locked onto the photographs, her thoughts racing through the possibilities. It was increasingly evident that the convergence of these experts held the sinister promise of a weaponized virus—a deadly concoction poised to be unleashed on a massive scale. The Super Bowl, an event that drew thousands of spectators, was the ideal target for such a catastrophic attack. The implications were staggering, the potential loss of life and chaos immeasurable. They were looking at the release of a deadly virus in a contained stadium. Once those in attendance who weren't killed left the stadium, they would be carriers. A falling domino scenario would take place.

Jeannie felt a surge of urgency as Director Costello's words echoed in her mind. She realized the clock was ticking and the need for action was imperative. The realization hit her like a wave of cold dread, but with it came a determination to uncover the truth, to thwart this nefarious plan before it could claim innocent lives.

Turning to Ismail, she saw the same understanding in his eyes, the same realization of the impending danger. Their unspoken connection spoke volumes, a shared commitment to unraveling the layers of deception and preventing the unimaginable from occurring.

The room seemed to shrink around them as the depth of seriousness of the situation took hold. Jeannie knew time was of the essence, and every moment wasted could bring the nightmare scenario closer to reality. She met Director Costello's gaze with a firm resolve and uttered the words that set the course for their next steps, "We need to find out everything we can about these virologists, the Germans, and their plans. Lives are at stake, and we can't afford to let this unfold." The urgency in her voice mirrored that in her heart as they embarked on a race against time, determined to thwart a deadly plot that could reshape the world as they knew it.

"We need Interpol to dig hard but discreetly into Vogel, Germany's Chancellor. I feel he is definitely the mastermind behind all this," Jeannie said.

As they prepared to leave Costello's office, he added a final remark, his tone a mix of frustration and bewilderment. "It's not just my agency but also intelligence organizations across the globe that struggle to comprehend how your present administration permits such a free flow of evil-intended actors in and out of your country. Something seems amiss."

"Preaching to the choir," Ismail replied wryly, his hand gently closing Director Costello's office door.

Delaney cruised into the Aryan Vanguard bar's parking lot on his Harley, the distinct rumble of his chopper's engine fading as he switched it off. Inside, the air was thick with conversation and the clink of glasses. Jake sat on a stool at the bar, deeply engaged in a phone conversation amid the hubbub. Sean's presence caught Jake's attention as he strolled in. A subtle nod and a motion of his hand signaled Sean over, simultaneously conveying an order to the bartender to pour him a beer.

Sean noticed the shift in Jake's demeanor as the phone call continued. Snippets of conversation floated through the air, and Sean's instincts tingled, sensing something of significant import. Jake's normally steady voice held a certain gravity as he spoke into the phone.

"I got it," Jake's voice was forceful, his volume low. "Our group will be prepared. We'll execute the plan as instructed."

Sean's mind raced as the conversation continued, piecing together the puzzle before him. There was a sense of urgency, a mission, and Delaney's intuition began connecting the dots.

Finally, Jake ended the call, his gaze meeting Sean's as he sighed and leaned back on the stool. "You must be wondering," he began, his voice tinged with a mixture of frustration and helplessness, "but honestly, I don't know much more than you do." He paused, his fingers tapping lightly on the bar's surface. "All I've been told is that The Organization has some sort of event tied to the Super Bowl, and they want us to create a disturbance miles away. They want to divert the police from the main scene." He shook his head, a hint of exasperation in his expression. "I don't get all the details, just orders."

"What type of disturbance?" Delaney asked.

"Seems The Organization is spewing some serious shit on social media, riling up those pussy Antifa folks," Jake muttered, his disdain evident. "They're aiming for a good ol' gang brawl a few miles from here. Once those jerks appear all masked up, we'll serve 'em a well-deserved beatdown."

Sean couldn't suppress his concern. "But what if we get caught in the crossfire? I mean, the cops won't let it spiral out of control, right?"

Jake's wry smile held a mix of cynicism and grim understanding. "You're still a bit green here, my friend. Back in the day, you'd be on the money. Cops would charge in, and it'd be a chaotic free-for-all. But these days, with all the 'defund the police' nonsense, they're often told to hang back. Let the dust settle if you will. Our little showdown could go on for a while; people might end up dead, cars torched, businesses looted. Pretty much the liberal utopia and just what The Organization is gunning for."

"Do you know what The Organization has planned for the Super Bowl?"

"Nah. Those fuckers only tell you what you need to know, but shit, as long as they send up money and guns, fuck 'em. Come on, have another beer."

TWENTY-ONE

A text message abruptly interrupted Delaney while he was composing another anonymous email to apprise the FBI of the impending possibility of several uprisings designed to divert law enforcement's attention from the stadium.

"SS Captain Franke and his spouse, Greta, resided deep in the Brazilian jungle. Your intuition was on point; they had a son. Unfortunately, both Franke and Greta have been discovered deceased, and their son, now in his twenties, has vanished without a trace. This intel is somewhat outdated."

Delaney read the message twice, his mind grappling with the unsettling information it conveyed. A question materialized in his thoughts, demanding consideration. How could a mere infant, a clone birthed on Dr. Hausser's secluded island, have matured into his twenties by now? The discrepancy was puzzling, leading him to speculate. Could it be that Dr. Hausser had initiated the creation of Hitler clones earlier than previously assumed?

Jeannie and Ismail were waylaid by Lomax in the bustling hallway on their return to the bureau from their Interpol meeting. He held a printout of the most recent anonymous email, his expression a mix of seriousness and anticipation. Ismail and Jeannie took turns scanning the contents and absorbing its implications.

"The Organization is formulating plans with various neo-Nazi groups to simultaneously create chaos in streets away from the Super Bowl site to draw manpower from the stadium. Still working on what The Organization has planned."

"We've got to head to Phoenix immediately," Jeannie urged, her excitement palpable. "Could you coordinate with the local agencies down there? Just send them an alert that's a bit more discreet, something like "remain vigilant for potential civil unrest stemming from..." You know, enough to give them a heads up without raising The Organization's suspicions."

Lomax nodded, his understanding clear. "Consider it done," he affirmed, his focus on the task ahead. The seriousness of the situation hung in the air, their urgent steps toward unraveling the sinister plot growing ever more critical.

Vogel sat at his desk, engrossed in analyzing action reports streaming in from Organization members across the globe. The power of social media had been harnessed to an alarming extent, successfully indoctrinating millions of impressionable young minds into the folds of National Socialism.

This manipulation had ignited civil unrest in some nations, each turmoil orchestrated by The Organization with a calculated hand. The ultimate outcome seemed almost inconsequential since Vogel held the reins that steered their fate. Soon, their allegiance would be sworn to the Nazi Party, or they would simply fade from the equation, eradicated without remorse.

Vogel motioned for Schneider, Wagner, and Werner to enter. They saluted with a resounding "Heil Hitler" as they stepped into the room, their arms raised in unison. Vogel acknowledged their salute by raising his hand in return, his gaze fixed on each of them as though he were probing the depths of their loyalty. "What news do you bring?" he inquired.

"Mein Führer," Schneider spoke, his voice firm. "Our rendezvous with our Chinese counterparts was successful. They provided the necessary materials destined for the stadium. Our operatives are discreetly installing the viral distribution devices right now within the air conditioning units across the entire facility. A wireless command will activate the dispersal process. Those within the stadium's interior will remain oblivious to the virus' dissemination."

"Excellent," Vogel remarked, his anticipation evident as he awaited further updates.

"In addition, orchestrated acts of civil disruption will ignite preceding the event, diverting focus and draining the emergency response forces. The political climate is conducive to such turmoil, given the schism between the Republican and Democrat parties," Schneider elaborated.

"And which faction shall we align with?" Vogel inquired, removing his reading glasses from the bridge of his nose and placing them deliberately on his desk. "Ultimately, it hardly matters, for whether it's the red or blue that drives America into a state of internal conflict, our initial support will fuel both sides. Once the dust settles, we shall mold the victorious into devoted adherents of the Fourth Reich."

"Indeed, Mein Führer. Our intelligence indicates a prevailing likelihood of the Conservative Party's triumph, which will inevitably lead to the subjugation of the liberal faction. Our projections foresee the defeated party being initially confined to internment facilities until their minds are recalibrated to embrace the principles of National Socialism. By extending our support to the victors, the process of indoctrination will likely unfold more seamlessly," Schneider declared, his tone infused with self-assured pride.

Jeannie and Ismail, joined by Burk and Darcy, occupied the breakroom, savoring slices of pizza thoughtfully provided by Jeannie. Amid this mealtime collaboration, Jeannie efficiently ensured her team members destined for Arizona were thoroughly prepared for their imminent departure, a mere two hours away.

Drawn not only by the enticing scent of the pizza but also by the pressing weight of a third anonymous email, Lomax entered the room with a determined stride, his demeanor akin to that of a man fervently on a mission.

"Yet another email," Lomax remarked, placing a printed copy of the communication on the table before helping himself to a slice of pizza. "Unfortunately, it doesn't bring much new to the table."

With anticipation in the air, Jeannie took the lead in perusing the email's contents, Ismail standing beside her to gain a glimpse.

"Three Chinese virologists, Ming Tao, Zhi Peng, and Chao-Xing, arrived on-site at the State Farm Stadium in Glendale, Arizona," the email detailed. "I personally witnessed them exchanging boxes with Herrs Schneider, Wagner, and Werner from The Organization. The contents of these boxes remain unknown. The virologists seemed to be providing instructions to the German trio before their departure."

"Once the virologists exited, the German associates convened with other suspected members of The Organization and transferred the boxes into the facility. Evidently, whatever is in motion seems to be approaching its final stages. Latterly, I confirmed the three Chinese scientists have flights from Arizona back to China."

"Damn," Ismail exclaimed, his admiration evident. "This individual has skills. I'd say they could make it as a top-tier FBI agent, just like me."

Lomax's reaction bordered on a mock choking fit, prompting Ismail to hastily interject, having momentarily forgotten Lomax's presence. "I mean, I'm just messing around, sir."

A smile graced Jeannie's lips as she retrieved the email copy from Burk and Darcy, ready to contribute to the conversation.

"You're absolutely right," Jeannie mused. "This person possesses an uncanny ability to blend in and become a true chameleon within their surroundings to glean such valuable intelligence. The depth of their investigative acumen must be remarkable. There's another intriguing angle. The fact that our informant is unaware of our prior knowledge about the virologists suggests a potential lack of connections to Interpol."

"Well, whoever this guy is," Ismail began to say...

"Or woman," Darcy interjected.

"Exactly, or woman," Ismail corrected himself, "whoever they are, they've essentially underlined the pressing need for us to infiltrate the stadium and uncover whatever might have been planted there. With the major event just around the corner, time is running short."

TWENTY-TWO

Jeannie's team, a mix of seasoned FBI agents and skilled specialists, arrived in Arizona with a sense of urgency hanging in the air. The sun's warm embrace did little to lighten the weight of the task at hand. Glendale was bustling with the energy that only a major sporting event could evoke, but the backdrop of their mission loomed large.

As Jeannie and her team touched down, they had a brief encounter with Rizzo, the ATF liaison, at the airport. A tall man with a no-nonsense demeanor, Rizzo greeted them with a firm handshake.

"Welcome to Arizona," he greeted, his words resonating with a seamless blend of professional courtesy and camaraderie. "Didn't we just put a stop to some terrorist plots over in Las Vegas?" Rizzo quipped, a friendly grin spreading across his face as he gave Ismail a hearty pat on the back.

His jest harkened back to a recent collaboration where they had thwarted the efforts of three terrorists who had a peculiar obsession with targeting roller coasters at amusement parks. Two targets were bombed with numerous casualties. Then, while the third terrorist was planning to blow up an indoor roller coaster at a new amusement park in Las Vegas, the other two had been aiming for the Skywalk over the Grand Canyon before meeting their demise at the hands of Jeannie and Rizzo. The third terrorist was dispatched after Jeannie and Rizzo caught him.

Rizzo's comment hung in the air, a reminder of their shared victories and an understanding of their significant accomplishments and the past woven into their camaraderie.

Their accommodations weren't the usual cozy hotels. With the Super Bowl days away, enthusiasts and football fanatics already occupied the closest lodgings. Rizzo had managed to secure arrangements at a National Guard post in Glendale. It wasn't the most glamorous option, but it was strategically suitable in its proximity to the State Farm Stadium.

The meeting convened once everyone settled into the alliance formed under the banner of security, comprising Jeannie and her team, Rizzo with his ATF associates, and meticulously vetted individuals from the NFL security.

Jeannie's commanding and engaging voice set the tone for the discussion. "We're facing a unique challenge here," she began, her gaze sweeping across the assembled group. "Time is a luxury we don't have. The clock is ticking down to the Super Bowl, and we need to make sure there's no potential threat looming within those walls."

Rizzo nodded in agreement, his expression serious. "We've got some top-notch experts on our side, and our primary focus is ensuring the safety of everyone attending that event."

An NFL security representative, Steve Lawson, a stout man with a demeanor that conveyed a lifetime of experience, chimed in. "We've combed through our ranks, ensuring every member involved in event security has passed rigorous background checks."

Jeannie leaned forward, her tone contemplative, "Given the timeline, we can't extend the same vetting process to the local law enforcement agencies. So, here's what I propose." She outlined a plan to covertly enter the stadium under cover of night, employing the expertise of the teams assembled around the table. The goal was clear: identify any anomalies or potential threats planted by The Organization.

Rizzo leaned back, considering the proposition. "It's a bold move, but with the event looming, we can't afford to wait."

The NFL security director nodded in agreement. "Agreed. And with our collective skills, we can ensure that this Super Bowl is remembered for the game, not for any sinister disruptions."

"Before we wrap up, ladies and gentlemen, there's one crucial detail to address," Jeannie announced, her tone carrying a weight of importance. "A few years back, my team and I tracked down an urban terrorist cell with plans to release a deadly gas into a similar venue, targeting attendees of the Democratic National Convention. Thankfully, we managed to intercept the weaponized vials before their lethal contents could be unleashed."

"As we're facing suspects with backgrounds in virology, particularly the Chinese virologists in question," Jeannie continued, "our primary concern should be the ventilation systems. We're in the dark about the exact nature of the virus they might plan to deploy, so if you come across anything suspicious, alert either Rizzo or me immediately. And I can't emphasize this enough: under no circumstances should you attempt to handle any device."

The Arizona sun had not yet set as the meeting concluded, but the intensity of their mission illuminated the path ahead.

Jeannie, Ismail, Burk, and Darcy gathered at a quaint eatery just a stone's throw from the National Guard station. Jeannie's mind seemed to wander, lost in contemplation as the menu lay open before her.

Observing her distant expression, Ismail was quick to inquire, his tone laced with concern, "What's on your mind, boss lady?" he asked, his food choice already determined. "Word on the street is that their wings are exceptional. Everything okay?"

She smiled and looked around the table at her friends, grateful for the concern. "Yeah, I'm fine," she replied, taking a sip of her soda. "I was just reminiscing about a mission we had a while back. Remember that time we had to locate those deadly gas containers at the Democratic National Convention site?"

Ismail's eyes lit up as he leaned in closer and said, "Oh, yeah, I remember that one. That was a tough nut to crack. But we managed to pull it off just in the nick of time, right before the leader of The Sons and Daughters of Liberty attempted to activate them."

Burk nodded in agreement, his expression serious. "That was a close call. Those containers were hidden so strategically that if we hadn't been able to find them, the consequences could have been catastrophic."

Darcy chimed in, a hint of pride in her voice, "And let's not forget, we not only located the containers but also captured their leader. That was a major win for us and the safety of the convention attendees. Justice played out when he was killed by fellow inmates while doing his life sentence."

As Jeannie shared this memory with her friends, she couldn't help but feel a surge of camaraderie. These people had stood by her side through thick and thin, facing danger and uncertainty together. However, her thoughts weren't limited to just that mission.

"Speaking of dangerous situations," she continued, her tone growing somber, "I've also been thinking about Sean Delaney, the Interpol agent. You remember him, right? He was killed in that booby trap inside the abandoned missile silo in Japan," she looked at Ismail, Burk, and Darcy. "The three of you probably didn't know that Sean and I were an item. Who knows where our relationship might have gone?"

Ismail's brows furrowed as he recalled the name. "Yeah, I remember 007. It was a tragic loss. But why are you thinking about him now? I mean, it's been some time."

Jeannie sighed, her gaze distant. "Well, you know those anonymous emails we've been receiving lately, the ones hinting at some sort of threat? I can't shake the feeling that they might be connected to Delaney, even though Interpol confirmed his death."

Ismail exchanged a concerned look with the others. "That's quite a leap, Jeannie. If he was confirmed dead, how could he be behind those emails?"

Jeannie nodded, acknowledging the skepticism. "I know it sounds far-fetched, but I can't ignore my nagging suspicion. Delaney was known for his skills in deception and manipulation. Maybe he faked his death somehow. I just think we need to tread carefully and consider all possibilities."

Her friends fell silent, absorbing her words. They had been through enough unexpected twists and turns in their line of work to understand that nothing was ever truly certain. As they sat, sipping their sodas and beer, lost in thought, Jeannie's mind continued to race, the pieces of the puzzle slowly coming together in her head.

TWENTY-THREE

The countdown to the pivotal event was in full swing, with only 48 hours remaining until the long-awaited big game. The anticipation was palpable, an electric charge that seemed to infuse the air itself. Jeannie's heart raced as she entered a sprawling tent, an impressive structure the National Guard had hurriedly erected to accommodate Rizza and Jeannie's teams. The atmosphere inside was thick with nervous energy and determination.

There was a hive of activity within as it bustled with agents and operatives from various agencies, all united under Rizzo's and her leadership. Jeannie couldn't help but be struck by the camaraderie and shared purpose that seemed to bind this diverse group of individuals. It was a testament to the seriousness of the mission at hand.

Jeannie's eyes swept over the crowd as she stepped further into the tent. Every seat was occupied, and every inch of space was claimed. The room seemed to vibrate with the hushed conversations of people preparing, strategizing, and readying themselves for what lay ahead. She glanced at her wristwatch, illuminated in the dim light. It displayed 1 a.m. The minutes slipped away like grains of sand through an hourglass.

Jeannie found solace in the company of her trusted comrades Ismail, Burk, and Darcy, along with the rest of her dedicated team members. A sense of unity was evident among the assemblage of officers and agents, manifesting itself in the jerseys worn by many of those present. Jerseys representing their favorite teams adorned the shoulders of the individuals about to embark on a critical mission. Jeannie had also fully embraced the spirit of the occasion amid this sea of companionship. She had donned a San Francisco 49ers jersey, the iconic red and gold fabric emblazoned with the number 16 on the front and back. This numerical choice held a profound significance—it was the number famously sported by none other than her all-time favorite Niner, Joe Montana.

As the countdown continued and the tension mounted, Jeannie's seemingly incongruous choice of attire spoke volumes about the depth of her connection to the moment and the shared passion uniting everyone present. The jersey wasn't just a piece of clothing; it was also a symbol of devotion to a cause, a testament to the unbreakable bond that was forged through their shared dedication to their mission.

With every passing minute, the jersey-clad individuals stood on the precipice of action, their collective determination shimmering like a beacon in the night. Jeannie's choice to honor the legacy of Joe Montana served as a testament to the power of inspiration, even in the face of daunting challenges. It was a reminder that sometimes, even amid the gravest situations, a touch of camaraderie and the embrace of shared symbols could lend strength to one's resolve.

They would execute the next phase of their plan in just a quarter of an hour, making their move into the stadium under the cover of darkness. The vital elements of stealth and precision couldn't be overstated. The NFL security head had meticulously ensured that only thoroughly vetted personnel remained within the confines of the stadium. The careful screening was meant to eliminate any potential threats, but Jeannie knew that The Organization, their elusive and formidable adversary, was always one step ahead.

She caught glimpses of familiar faces as her eyes scanned the room, agents she had worked with on various missions. There was a reassuring familiarity in their presence, a shared history that spoke of the dangers they had faced together and the bonds they had formed under fire. The stakes were higher than ever, and the weight of responsibility hung heavy in the air.

The delicate balance between success and failure was at play. One wrong move, one unforeseen detail, and The Organization would catch wind that their meticulous plan had been discovered. The tension was a living entity, a silent undercurrent beneath the surface of every whispered conversation and every exchanged glance.

Jeannie found herself lost in thought as the minutes ticked away, reflecting on the journey that had led them to this pivotal moment. The sacrifices, the late-night strategy sessions, and the painstaking planning had all culminated in this juncture. The realization that they were on the precipice of potentially unraveling a network of deceit and danger was exhilarating and sobering in equal measure.

The tent hummed with a sense of unity, purpose, and the shared understanding that they were undertaking something far greater than themselves. They were the last line of defense against a shadowy threat that had woven itself into the very fabric of society. And as the clock continued to count down, Jeannie steeled herself for what lay ahead, determined to seize the opportunity to make a difference, even in the face of overwhelming odds.

Before long, a fleet of buses pulled up at the tent's entrance, their engines humming as if in anticipation. Rizzo's voice rang out amid the mounting excitement, cutting through the air with clear instructions. "No need to worry about which bus you board," he announced to the assembled group, "simply find a seat for the brief journey to the stadium. Once we arrive, link up with your designated team leader. And yes, this applies to our FBI partners as well."

Rizzo's words carried an air of authority and purpose, underscoring their mission's importance. The intricate web of coordination was further revealed as Jeannie continued, outlining their NFL colleagues' specific roles. "For those from the NFL, you will be stationed at each of the facility's entry points. Your task is to ensure no one gains access behind us," she directed, her gaze sweeping across the diverse assembly.

A note of preparedness laced Rizzo's next words as he stressed the significance of their covert operation. "Remember, each of you has been equipped with a cover story in case the need arises," he reminded, his tone steady and reassuring. The intense significance of their mission was evident, requiring skill and the ability to adapt in the face of the unforeseen.

The call to action resonated through the tent, a chorus of unity that transcended affiliations and backgrounds. With a final nod to the shared purpose uniting them all, Rizzo's voice carried a sense of urgency. "Alright, everyone, let's move out. And please, exercise caution every step of the way." His words hung in the air, a reminder of the stakes they were playing for and the imperative to approach their task with unwavering focus and vigilance. He looked at Jeannie, and they extended a nod to each other.

TWENTY-FOUR

The anticipation was almost palpable as the assembled team, led by Rizzo and Jeannie and comprising Ismail, Darcy, Burk, and a cohort of officers, made their way into the colossal stadium. The cavernous expanse that normally held roaring crowds was now eerily silent, a canvas of excitement waiting to burst forth.

The space was transformed, adorned in the grandeur of championship fervor. Banners fluttered from the rafters, team flags waving like determined sentinels of competition. The opposing teams' names blazed across the end zones in a visual representation of the imminent showdown.

As they ventured deeper into the stadium, the atmosphere seemed to hold its breath, laden with both the intensity of their mission and the spectacle that was about to unfold. Every footfall echoed in the vastness, each heartbeat resonating with the magnitude of their task. Rizzo's keen eyes scanned the surroundings, his expression a blend of focused determination and a readiness for the unexpected.

The initial minutes of their search were charged with suspense, each member of the team methodically combing through the labyrinthine corridors, checking every nook and cranny. The weight of the mission seemed to hang in the air, a tangible force propelling them forward. Jeannie's senses were heightened, her years of training guiding her every step as she carefully swept her surroundings with a watchful eye.

Time seemed to stretch as the minutes ticked by, a crescendo of tension building with every moment that passed. During these painstaking minutes, an agent, his gloved hands inspecting an unassuming air conditioning unit, experienced a jolt of discovery. The group's feeling of intensity was raised to the highest level as he could just see a vial deep inside an A/C unit that had been missed. The contents and purpose were unknown, but his discovery sent a surge of hope through the group.

The team swiftly went into action, calling in a maintenance crew to carefully dismantle the A/C unit. Jeannie ordered all the other A/C units to be inspected again.

The task at hand demanded precision and caution, the stakes too high for even the slightest misstep. As each piece of the unit was disassembled, the truth was unveiled: a vial containing a deadly viral concoction was nestled within the machine's inner workings.

Shock and alarm rippled through the group, a stark reminder of the sinister intent they were up against.

The discovery prompted an immediate reassessment of the situation, and a secondary sweep was initiated. The team used flashlights and discovered each A/C unit in the same location held a similar vial.

The seconds stretched into minutes as the team painstakingly checked and rechecked to ensure no other devices lay hidden, the collective resolve unwavering in the face of the unknown.

Eventually, their exhaustive search yielded the relief they had been hoping for: no other devices were found. The tension that had gripped them began to loosen its hold, replaced by a sense of accomplishment and shared determination.

A total of fourteen ominous devices were successfully located and extracted from various points within the stadium's labyrinthine ventilation systems. With the immediate threat neutralized, Jeannie assumed the role of guiding presence. She addressed the collective assemblage in a hushed yet resolute tone, conveying her precise instructions. Everyone present was urged to meticulously backtrack their movements, leaving no trace of the exhaustive search that had taken place.

Everyone executed their task with quiet determination, methodically erasing any evidence of their painstaking investigation. The atmosphere was charged with a sense of purpose as they worked in synchrony, their shared commitment shining through in each careful action.

A collective breath seemed to release as the task was completed, marking a turning point in the mission. With the stadium now secured, its very essence seemed to mirror the team's readiness. The NFL security director, aware of the ongoing activity, issued explicit directives. Monitoring cameras were to remain fixed on every air conditioning unit, their unwavering gaze continuing well beyond the culmination of the championship game.

"We're in a waiting game now," Jeannie remarked to Rizzo, her tone a blend of patience and anticipation.

Rizzo's response carried a hint of lightness, a respite from the tension that had gripped them. "At least we'll have a front-row seat for the main event," he quipped, a glimmer of amusement dancing in his eyes.

Ismail's playful smile interjected with a touch of good-natured banter, "You know, considering the effort we just put in, maybe the NFL will surprise us with a luxury box."

A wry chuckle escaped Jeannie's lips, her eyes conveying a mix of exasperation and fondness as she looked at Ismail. Meanwhile, Rizzo burst into a hearty laugh, the sound echoing through the corridors and briefly lightening the weight of their circumstances.

The much-anticipated day finally dawned—the day of the big game. The stadium, now teeming with thousands of excited fans, was a vibrant tapestry of color, fervor, and anticipation. Jeannie and Rizzo had orchestrated a meticulous plan, deploying their agents throughout the venue in various covert roles, including ticket takers, souvenir vendors, and more. The agents blended seamlessly with the crowd, their faces determined yet unassuming, ready to intercept any threat that might arise.

Jeannie and Ismail assumed their roles as seemingly ordinary security guards amid the sea of fans, their every move calculated and vigilant. They patrolled the premises with practiced ease, eyes scanning for any anomalies or potential dangers that might disrupt the event.

Meanwhile, Darcy and Burk took their positions in the control room, their focus trained on the intricate web of NFL cameras that spanned the stadium. Their vigilant gaze reached every corner and every angle in search of any sign of irregularity.

As the hours passed, the stadium atmosphere began to swell with excitement, a palpable energy that charged the air. A few unruly individuals crossed the line amid the crowd's buzz, leading to their arrest by the local law enforcement team stationed at the event. Swift action was taken to defuse any flare-ups and maintain a sense of order amid the spectacle.

Jeannie just shook her head before yelling at Ismail, "Can you believe these idiots pay over $1,000 to see the game and then get too drunk to enjoy it?"

"I didn't notice; I was watching the cheerleaders." Jeannie hit Ismail on his shoulder.

Yet another incident caught Darcy and Burk's attention as they monitored the cameras. A figure loitering near an A/C unit raised suspicion, prompting them to investigate further. Their suspicions were quickly allayed; however, as it turned out, the individual was merely indulging in a casual joint. The momentary lapse in tension drew a knowing chuckle from the control room, a small reminder that amid the calculated vigilance, the unexpected could sometimes be amusing.

Jeannie's phone buzzed amid this dynamic environment, signaling an incoming call. It was Lomax on the other end, his voice steady and authoritative. As anticipated, he relayed the news that several clashes had erupted between neo-Nazis and left-wing fanatics, confirming their intelligence and expectations. The situation was swiftly contained, a testament to the arious teams interwoven efforts to ensure security and order.

The heightened vigilance bore fruit as the game played out on the field, yielding a relatively incident-free event. The crowd roared with excitement, encapsulating the fervor of competition, while behind the scenes, the invisible protectors ensured the threat they had uncovered remained contained. The culmination of the game came and went without disruption, a testament to the expertise, teamwork, and relentless dedication of those who had orchestrated its safety.

The enigma of the benefactor behind the extensive array of food and beverages set up in the expansive tent after everyone returned from the stadium remained shrouded from Rizzo. However, Ismail was privy to their identity, and he exchanged a sly wink with Jeannie, the shared secret evident in their eyes.

Rizzo's genuine astonishment colored his words as he took in the sight before him. "Incredible," he exclaimed. "Can you believe the sheer amount of food and drinks they've laid out?"

Jeannie's response carried a hint of pride in a quiet acknowledgment of the team's well-deserved indulgence. "Absolutely," she replied, her gaze sweeping the tent. A veil of calmness draped her demeanor, masking the fact that she had a hand in orchestrating this generous gesture.

She moved around the spread casually, the array of food and beverages beckoning invitingly. Her seemingly ordinary actions belied the fact that she was the architect behind the arrangement, a reflection of her appreciation for the teams' hard work and dedication. Her face remained unflustered even as she partook in the feast she had organized, her composure a testament to her ability to remain incognito.

TWENTY-FIVE

WOLF'S LAIR

The parking area teemed with multiple black vehicles, their sinister presence creating an intimidating atmosphere. Nazi flags, caught by the breeze, fluttered momentarily before resuming their stern positions. Clad in impeccably black uniforms and gleaming boots, several SS guards strategically patrolled the compound's perimeter. A formidable presence of guards was stationed at the stairway's entrance that led beneath the Wolf's Lair's ancient structure to the newer section.

Warmth emanated from the congregation of numerous Nazi members within the main briefing chamber, many adorned in their uniforms. A colossal Nazi flag draped along the back wall dominated the space, while the opposite wall showcased a majestic golden eagle in all its grandeur.

Vogel strode briskly into the room, an aura of urgency accompanying his arrival. The assembled individuals swiftly straightened, their voices harmonizing in a resounding "Heil Hitler," accompanied by the synchronized clicking of their boots slamming against each other. Curiously, the Hitler clone refrained from reciprocating the salute, a detail that did not escape many discerning eyes. He cradled his left arm with noticeable discomfort, although he maintained his posture. He was attired in a brown sports jacket and the emblematic armband. His focus fell upon the disarray of papers scattered across the expanse of the imposing oak table. An unsettling hush enveloped the room, each occupant keenly attuned to the atmosphere as it became apparent that the Führer was in a far from favorable disposition.

"Back on the 20th of July in 1944, my father occupied the very spot where I stand today, except he was elevated, positioned just above me. Colonel Stauffenberg and a group of treacherous officers from the Third Reich plotted his assassination at that time." He paused, allowing his words to linger in the air before proceeding.

"My father's trust in his command staff was his vulnerability, a trust that was cruelly betrayed by those spineless traitors. His mistake led to his downfall. His fatal error was allowing someone to encroach too intimately and be privy to the revelation of his innermost thoughts."

He attempted to bring clarity to the words before him as he adjusted his reading glasses. However, an uncontrollable tremor in his left hand caused him to gingerly remove his glasses using his steadier right hand. He inadvertently dropped the spectacles onto the document spread before him.

" My father persisted in heeding the generals who spun webs of deceit, feeding him fabricated tales of resistance against the encroaching forces, even as the enemy tightened their grip. Oh, indeed, they skillfully wove a tapestry of falsehoods to cloud his judgment. They were driven by their self-preservation, their hearts never truly devoted to the Fatherland as my father's was."

Vogel's agitation escalated, evident in the beads of moisture forming around his mouth that were expelled forcefully as he spoke, the tension reverberating across the table.

"Herr Schneider," his voice sliced through the room, and Schneider snapped to attention. "Yes, Mein Führer," he responded promptly.

"Would you care to enlighten us all about your endeavor's outcome—the attack on the Americans as they celebrated their championship football game?" The question hung heavily in the air.

Schneider was visibly uneasy as sweat began to bead on his collar while rivulets traced down his cheeks. His voice trembled as he responded, "Mein Führer, it is with great regret that I must report that American law enforcement uncovered our operation. A female FBI agent, Loomis, together with American Alcohol, Tobacco, and Firearms found the virus vials and removed them. Regrettably, none of the devices we meticulously planted in the building could be activated. I…"

The Hitler clone waved him off before he could finish his sentence. He then slammed both his fists on the large table, and his glasses jumped due to the vibration.

As Vogel's words surged forth, they carried a current of fervor that electrified the room. His voice grew louder, fueled by a torrent of emotion that had long been suppressed. The atmosphere tightened, each syllable he uttered resonating like an ominous drumbeat. Rage simmered beneath the surface, finally breaking free from the chains that had confined it.

His hands clenched into fists at his sides, and the veins at his temples pulsed in rhythm with his escalating fury. The air seemed to thicken with every moment, a palpable tension radiating from Vogel's very being. The others in the room exchanged uneasy glances, the weight of his anger hanging heavy in the air.

Vogel's pacing grew more erratic, his movements almost frenzied. He strode across the room, his voice reaching a crescendo and words tumbling from his lips like molten lava. His eyes blazed with a mixture of intense anger and a profound sense of betrayal. The echo of his accusations reverberated off the walls in a tempest of emotion that seemed to engulf everyone present.

Minutes stretched like an eternity as Vogel's rage spiraled further, his grip on control slipping away like sand through clenched fingers. It was a storm of emotions, the tempestuous culmination of years of simmering discontent and desire for retribution. Once composed and controlled, his demeanor had morphed into something altogether more frightening.

Schneider, the man under the weight of Vogel's ire, felt beads of sweat forming on his forehead amid this maelstrom of fury. The intensity of Vogel's anger was overwhelming, its force radiating outward. Schneider's fingers trembled slightly, his fear mingling with the anxiety that pervaded the room. As Vogel's tirade continued unabated, Schneider discreetly pulled out a handkerchief and wiped the sweat from his brow, his gesture a fleeting moment of respite amid the tumultuous scene.

Vogel's rage showed no sign of abating. His voice continued to cascade through the room like a relentless tempest, each word etching his fury into the very walls. The others watched on, witnesses to a storm that had been unleashed, a storm that left them simultaneously captivated and terrified.

Then, in an abrupt and chilling turn, Vogel's fury manifested into action. Without warning, he swiftly produced a gleaming semi-automatic from his holster. Standing close behind Schneider, Vogel's finger squeezed the trigger, releasing a single round that tore through the short distance with deadly intent. The gunshot cracked like thunder in a jarring rupture that reverberated through the room, imprinting its echo upon the perimeter.

The bullet struck its mark with unforgiving precision, piercing the back of Schneider's head. The impact sent shockwaves through his body in an instant and brutal termination of life. Schneider's form crumpled to the floor.

Vogel did not initially look at the aftermath of his action. Instead, he casually walked around the body of Schneider and came face to face with Weber and Wagner. They stared at the large Nazi flag, terrified, attempting to avoid the Hitler clone's gaze.

The room, which had been a cauldron of Vogel's rage, was now transformed into a tableau of stunned silence. The sharp report of the gunshot still lingered in the air, its resonance a haunting reminder of the irreversible act that had just unfolded. Ears rang, and hearts raced, the aftermath of the shot leaving many temporarily disoriented, their senses momentarily dulled by the sonic assault.

Vogel's hand, which had delivered both judgment and death, remained steady at his side. His gaze, recently so ablaze with anger, now held an eerie calmness as he looked down at Schneider's fallen figure. The seconds stretched, each burdened with the weight of the irreversible deed that had transpired.

Whispers of disbelief and fear began to ripple through the assembled individuals as the room slowly emerged from the grip of shock. Vogel's action had severed the tension, which was now replaced with an atmosphere of grim realization. The once vibrant room was now tainted by the aftermath of violence that bore witness to the chilling reality that their world had been forever altered.

He stood before Weber and Wagner. Both anticipated being executed. "Here before you lies a betrayer to the Fourth Reich. His inability to execute my command and strike at the Americans has turned us into a mockery in the eyes of Communist China. Does every individual in this room comprehend the strenuous effort I've invested in nurturing a cordial rapport with the Chinese? An inferior race. A nation we are inevitably destined to conquer. Consider their apprehension now, having witnessed our faltering in this endeavor."

Vogel appeared to be spent. He walked around to where he had been standing during his tirade. After regaining his composure, he again looked directly at Weber and Wagner. I am ordering you to find this FBI agent, Loomis, who discovered our plan. I want her executed immediately. Do you understand?"

TWENTY-SIX

Jeannie expressed her gratitude to her entire team once they returned to the bureau after their flight from Arizona. Ismail paused before getting into his car as he walked side by side with Jeannie in the secure garage where their vehicles were parked.

"I realize that case took a toll on you. Memories of the old 007 came back to me, too," he began. "But, boss, you and Rizzo pulled it off. The severity of the situation hit me as I thought about the countless lives that might have been lost if we hadn't intercepted that virus in time. I guess I'm trying to say congratulations without going all Hallmark on you."

"Thanks, Ace. That means a lot. Have a safe drive, and I'll catch you here tomorrow. By the way, I've arranged for your favorite breakfast catering service to be here at 9:30 a.m. to whip up a hearty morning feast for the whole team. You all definitely earned it."

"Wow! I better head home and thaw some linguica from the freezer. Those guys sure know how to grill it to perfection. See you bright and early in the morning."

Jeannie revved up her Corvette's engine and eased onto Highway 101 South, heading toward the Dumbarton Bridge. Despite her efforts, she couldn't suppress thoughts of Sean, and they grew more persistent the harder she tried. Giving in, she switched on her car radio and tuned into her preferred talk show. Her shock that followed was palpable as the news unfolded: Germany had mobilized its troops and positioned them ominously along the Polish border.

Jeannie Loomis stood before her team gathered in a conference room at their San Francisco headquarters as the morning sun painted the sky with shades of orange and pink. Her gaze swept across the faces she had come to know so well, each a testament to their dedication and resilience. With a warm smile, she began to speak.

"Team, I want you all to know how incredibly proud I am of each and every one of you," Jeannie's voice carried a mix of gratitude and determination. "The past few months have been a whirlwind, and you've faced challenges head-on. From the day we uncovered the truth behind the clones to the recent threat against the Super Bowl, you've shown unwavering commitment to keeping our world safe.

"We've navigated treacherous waters, and because of your skills, your passion, and your unity, we've come out the other side. Together, we thwarted disaster and protected countless lives. You've proven time and again that nothing can stand in our way when we work together as a team."

A round of nods and appreciative glances were exchanged among the team. Jeannie's words resonated deeply, affirming their shared mission and the bond they had forged.

A flurry of activity outside the conference room caught their attention as the meeting concluded. The aroma of sizzling bacon, freshly brewed coffee, and warm pastries wafted through the air. The caterers had arrived to cook breakfast for her team as a gesture of gratitude for their hard work and dedication.

Ismail Flores, Jeannie's friend and second in command, was the first to make his way to the table laden with breakfast delights. He grinned as he saw the spread, a touch of mischief in his eyes. "Hey, don't forget I brought something special from home," he said, holding up a package of linguica sausage.

Chuckling, the head caterer took the linguica links, "Ismail, you know you're always welcome to add your personal touch to our feasts."

Jeannie watched as her team members chatted and laughed, enjoying the respite they so deserved. Lomax entered the room with a warm smile just as they began to indulge in the delicious breakfast. "Well, it looks like I arrived just in time for the celebration," he said, his tone light-hearted.

Jeannie nodded with evident gratitude. "I can't thank you enough for your support and guidance throughout this journey. Your leadership has been instrumental in our success."

Lomax smiled with a proud expression. "You've all done exceptional work, Jeannie. It's a testament to your leadership and the extraordinary team you've assembled. Together, we've made a stand against those who would threaten our world."

Glancing over at Ismail, he observed the skilled hands of the cooks deftly preparing the Portuguese sausage. "I hear I can get some linguica with my scrambled eggs and hash browns," he remarked, a smile gracing his lips.

"Indeed, sir," Ismail replied, gesturing to the cook to serve some of his sausage alongside his boss's meal.

But the specter of danger still lingered in the shadows, unbeknownst to Jeannie and her team. It was a lurking reminder that their path ahead was fraught with challenges. Their subsequent moves would propel them deeper into a pivotal battle that could potentially determine the course of the world's destiny.

Weber and Wagner were greeted by two fellow members of The Organization as they exited San Francisco International Airport. Speaking in hushed tones in their native German, the front-seat passenger turned toward the duo, delivering the latest intelligence gathered from their surveillance on Jeannie.

"The first image depicts the imposing FBI headquarters," Erwin relayed, his youthful appearance belying the sharpness of his skills. "As anticipated, the security measures are substantial. The garage entrance is secured by a remotely operated metal gate."

Weber and Wagner's attention was fixed on the photograph, absorbing the details. "The subsequent picture captures Agent Loomis as she enters her sleek sports car, preparing to depart from the headquarters. We tracked her journey to a town named Newark,"

Erwin continued with a matter of fact tone, "And as evidenced in the following image, that's where her residence is situated. While there are signs indicating the presence of a Neighborhood Alert program, we didn't observe any overt security measures. This could be the opportune target point to strike."

TWENTY-SEVEN

Jeannie's early arrival at her home was an unexpected luxury, a respite granted by Lomax's insistence that she take an extended break. He and Ismail had taken charge of overseeing the catering crew, and Lomax had even hinted at the possibility of releasing everyone early as a token of his appreciation for their unflagging dedication.

With a quick stop at Safeway to gather the groceries she needed, Jeannie managed to slip into her garage, effectively evading any potential ambush by Delores. Once safely within the confines of her home, she stowed her perishables in the refrigerator before tending to her indoor and outdoor koi. The vibrant fish were in good health, their appetite evident as she fed them. Satisfied, she returned to the kitchen to organize the remaining groceries.

A soothing shower worked its magic on her tense shoulder muscles, and after slipping into a comfortable ensemble of well-worn sweatpants and a cozy pullover t-shirt, she nestled onto the couch near the kitchen. The TV was tuned to Newsmax, its familiar background noise creating a sense of comfort.

As Jeannie relaxed, her mind gradually drifted toward a dreamlike state. The final snippet of information that registered before sleep claimed her consciousness was the urgent announcement that the United Nations had called for an emergency meeting due to the unsettling presence of German troops gathering along the Polish border.

"That's her residence," Weber whispered to Wagner, even though they were in a vehicle. "Can't tell if anyone is home or not."

"According to Erwin, she usually arrives home by 6 p.m.," he noted, a glance at his watch confirming the time. "It's now 8:30, so she's either inside or out for the evening. Go around the side of the garage and check if the door's accessible or if we can manage to open it discreetly," Weber instructed, prompting Wagner to swiftly comply.

The absence of vigilant dogs in the vicinity meant his presence went unnoticed. He discovered the door to be locked, though he observed it sported a standard exterior lock susceptible to being picked or coerced open with a pair of channel locks. Wagner made his way back to the car and relayed his findings to Weber.

"Alright, let's clear out before arousing suspicion. We'll grab a late meal from a fast-food joint and then circle back to execute the plan. Erwin also mentioned her routine: she leaves the house around 6 a.m. for her commute. If we can access the garage tonight, we'll position the device and trigger it once she starts backing out of the driveway in the morning," Weber decided, the anticipation of the operation simmering in the air.

As instructed, Dr. Muller arrived at the Chancellor's office for his meeting with the Hitler clone. Upon being granted entry, he swiftly detected a noticeable shift in Vogel's physical demeanor. Dark circles accentuated his eye sockets, his posture exhibited a slight hunch, and his bloodshot eyes revealed signs of strain. An added concern was Vogel's left arm, which was cradled protectively against his chest.

Ensuring the door behind him was securely shut, he proceeded to perform the Hitler salute and accompanied it with a resounding "Heil Hitler" as he entered the room. Vogel's gaze lifted from his desk, his eyes appearing watery and fatigued. "Herr Doctor, I'm relieved you're here. As you can see, something is amiss. What did your tests uncover?"

Muller took a seat across from Vogel with an uneasy demeanor. "Mein Führer, would it be acceptable for me to commence with an examination?"

"Yes, yes. Get on with it," shouted an agitated Vogel. Muller meticulously assessed Vogel's condition, measuring his pulse, monitoring his blood pressure, testing his reflexes, and carefully observing his eyes and ears. Once his examination was complete and he had stowed his stethoscope in his medical bag, he gingerly settled into a chair. His trepidation about Vogel's reaction to the revelations weighed heavily on his mind.

Muller leaned forward, attempting to soften the impact of his message as he selected his words with the utmost care. "Mein Führer, I regret to inform you that the results did not align with our hopes." Vogel's left arm broke free from the clasp of his right, his distress evident as he instinctively cradled the afflicted limb once more.

"It seems that during the process of your creation at Dr. Hausser's facility, his primary focus was on incorporating an aging agent into your DNA. Regrettably, in doing so, he neglected to rectify the underlying health issues that afflicted your father—specifically, Parkinson's disease," Muller ventured, his voice carefully modulated as he conveyed the unsettling information.

A fraught pause hung in the air as he anxiously awaited a response from Vogel. However, it was evident that the Chancellor had become consumed by his thoughts, leaving Muller grappling with the tense silence.

After a prolonged moment of contemplation, Vogel eventually roused himself and gestured for Muller to continue. The anticipation and unease that had pervaded the room now took on a different form of an unsettling stillness underscored by the weight of the impending conversation.

Vogel's deep contemplation gave way to a firm nod, a tacit agreement for Muller to delve into the specifics. The doctor cleared his throat with a mixture of reluctance and a sense of duty before continuing. "Mein Führer, the aging agent in your DNA has, indeed, propelled your physiological age to 56 years old," Muller began, his tone weighted with the unfortunate nature of the revelation.

He paused, allowing the words to settle before elaborating further. "However, I must stress that the aging process is not without its consequences. We can anticipate a rapid progression of symptoms. Your posture will start to incline, and you may experience a shuffling gait when you walk." Muller's voice remained steady, yet the stark reality of the prognosis hung heavily in the air.

"Furthermore, the issues you've encountered with your left arm will likely worsen," he continued, his words measured. "Tremors will become more pronounced, affecting your ability to control movement. Your eyes may appear glassy and your skin greasier than before." Each detail was conveyed with clinical detachment, yet it carried an emotional weight that resonated in the room.

"In some instances, your speech may become barely audible," Muller continued, choosing his words with care. "The combined effects will likely present you as much older than your chronological age, Mein Führer. I'm sorry." The implications of his assessment were unmistakable, casting a stark light on the reality that lay ahead for Vogel.

As the weight of Vogel's impending condition settled upon the room, an unspoken question lingered in the air, one that mirrored the somber reality they were confronting. It was as if the room itself held its breath, awaiting the doctor's response to the hope-filled query.

Gathering himself, Muller recognized the unspoken concern that had surfaced. "Mein Führer, you must be wondering about potential treatments for Parkinson's disease," he ventured, acknowledging the unasked question that had hung in their midst.

Muller continued, his tone marked by a blend of clinical knowledge and empathy, "There are various approaches to managing the symptoms of Parkinson's today. Medications are often prescribed to help control tremors, improve motor skills, and maintain a level of cognitive function." He emphasized the importance of these medications in providing a measure of relief for those grappling with the disease's challenges.

"In addition," Muller went on, "physical therapy and regular exercise can help maintain mobility and manage muscle stiffness. Speech therapy may assist in mitigating difficulties with communication." He was careful to outline the range of options available, each aimed at enhancing Vogel's quality of life in the face of the inevitable progression.

However, Muller's voice carried a tinge of realism. "I must be forthright, Mein Führer. While these approaches can provide relief and manage symptoms to a certain extent, they cannot reverse the course of the disease." His words hung in the air, a testament to the limitations that medicine grappled with when confronting such complex ailments.

The room fell into a momentary silence, the weight of the prognosis and the understanding of its implications palpable. The conversation had shifted from the bleak reality Vogel faced to the broader landscape of medical science's ongoing pursuit of solutions. As they navigated this difficult terrain, the doctor's expertise served as a guide through the complexities of Parkinson's disease and the challenges it posed.

At last, Vogel emerged from his contemplative state, the weight of the grim prognosis noticeable in the air. It was as though his moment of introspection had been a necessary pause, allowing him to process the stark reality that had been laid before him.

"Thank you, Herr Doctor," his voice held a mixture of acceptance and determination. "My father had a physician he trusted, and I find myself fortunate to have you in my corner. We must begin the necessary treatments without delay."

His resolute tone conveyed the urgency that underscored his words, a recognition that time was of the essence. "The Fourth Reich's path forward hinges on my ability to lead them into this new era," Vogel continued, his commitment to his cause unwavering despite the personal challenges he was poised to face.

Muller listened, understanding the gravity of Vogel's words. The mantle of leadership weighed heavily upon him, and it was evident the Chancellor was prepared to face his health struggles in service of his vision. As they navigated this pivotal juncture, Muller couldn't help but marvel at the convergence of history, ideology, and the very real human experiences that shaped their decisions.

With a shared understanding of the path ahead, they now embarked on a journey that extended beyond medicine. The destiny of nations, the legacy of generations, and the intricacies of personal sacrifice were all bound up in the unfolding narrative. In that moment, Muller recognized that he was not merely a doctor attending to a patient; he was also a participant in a pivotal chapter of history, where the stakes were as high as they could be and where the course of events would be shaped by the choices they made in the face of adversity.

TWENTY-EIGHT

"What time is it?" Weber's voice quivered nervously as he took a sip from his coffee cup.

Consulting the dimly lit streetlights for reference, Wagner glanced at his watch and swiftly relayed his response. "It's 5:55. She should be preparing to leave her home." Almost as if on cue, the duo's attention was drawn to the gradual ascent of the garage door at Jeannie's residence.

"Get ready. As soon as she starts backing the car out, initiate the signal," Wagner's voice held a mixture of anticipation and urgency, reflecting the heightened emotions of the moment.

As Jeannie started backing her car out into the driveway, an unexpected realization struck her: she had forgotten to feed her fish. A surge of frustration and concern washed over her, prompting her to swiftly exit the vehicle. She hurriedly made her way toward the door of her home, her focus entirely on the indoor and outdoor koi that relied on her care.

Wagner's composure faltered as he observed Jeannie's abrupt movement. Panic set in as he processed the situation unfolding before him. The moment had arrived, the critical juncture they had meticulously planned for. With a trembling hand, he activated the signal that would set their plan into motion.

A jarring explosion shattered the early morning tranquility as the parked Corvette erupted into flames in the garage. The force of the blast reverberated, sending shockwaves through the structure. Flames licked at the structure, quickly consuming the space in a blazing inferno that seemed to mirror the chaos unfolding within their carefully constructed plot.

The once-sturdy front windows of Jeannie's home were no match for the shockwave, and their fragmentation echoed the violent impact. The cacophony of car alarms on the street joined the symphony of chaos, their shrill cries punctuating the air with discordant urgency.

The fire door separating the garage from the interior of Jeannie's home slammed shut with unexpected force, causing her to lose her balance and fall to the ground. The deafening sound of the explosion left her ears ringing amid the chaos, rendering her temporarily deaf. Gradually, the cacophony of blaring car horns pierced through the haze, the first semblance of audible sound that registered.

As Jeannie began to regain her bearings, her senses were assaulted by the unsettling crackling sounds emanating from the now-burning garage. The acrid scent of smoke and the faint hint of burning materials began to permeate the air. Her focus swiftly shifted to the fire door, the same barrier that had propelled her to the ground. It became clear that the very door that had protected her was now threatened by encroaching smoke and danger.

Jeannie acted swiftly with a surge of adrenaline. She reached for her cell phone and, with shaking hands, dialed 9-1-1, her voice a mixture of insistence and desperation as she relayed the unfolding emergency. Next, she dialed Lomax's number, her fingers tapping out the sequence with frantic determination. She placed the call and her voice trembled as she delivered the news to her superior. She knew every second counted as the flames consuming her garage threatened to spill over into her home.

She then managed to dial Ismail's number amid the chaos, the imperative in her actions mirrored by the urgency of her words. With each call, she sought to activate the network that would coordinate the appropriate response. Jeannie remained resolute as she navigated the tumultuous situation. She demonstrated the resourcefulness that had defined her actions throughout her storied career, even in the face of danger.

As the realization of their failure set in, Wagner and Weber were left with no choice but to swiftly withdraw. The plan that had been crafted with meticulous detail had unraveled in the span of moments. As the flames roared and the chaos reverberated, they scrambled to distance themselves from the disaster they had prematurely set in motion. With the weight of defeat heavy upon them, they retreated into the night, their dread a stark contrast to the anticipation that had fueled their ambitions.

The entire garage had been gutted by fire by the time the fire department arrived. The force of the water from their fire hoses only seemed to exacerbate the situation. The once gorgeous flaming red Corvette was reduced to the bottom frame and the still smoldering four tires.

Delores and Walter, the first neighbors at the scene, tried to comfort Jeannie, who, after experiencing the shock of the situation, wanted revenge. Upon learning from Jeannie what had happened, Lomax quickly phoned ATF assistant director Rizzo to send his best team to Jeannie's house. A $200,000 Corvette doesn't just blow up.

"What do we tell the Führer?" Weber's voice betrayed his unease, the weight of the disaster heavy on his shoulders.

"Nothing," Wagner's response was swift and decisive, reflecting the seriousness of the situation they faced. "If word reaches him that we've failed, the consequences will be dire—akin to Schneider's fate, or perhaps even worse, we'll meet our end suspended from piano wire somewhere." The awful truth of his words hung in the air, a stark reminder of the high-stakes world they operated within.

"No, we must act swiftly to devise an alternate strategy to eliminate her," Wagner's words carried a sense of urgency and a determination to rectify their failure and salvage their standing. "Should the Führer hear of our misstep, we'll counter with a well-crafted narrative, labeling the information as a false rumor. And we'll demonstrate, beyond a doubt, that Agent Loomis has met her demise."

Delaney leaned against the bar, nursing a cold beer in the dimly lit confines of the Aryan Vanguard hangout. The joint was pretty quiet at first, with only a couple of other members shooting pool. The low rumble of conversation created a backdrop to the atmosphere, hinting at the edgy camaraderie shared among the outlaw brotherhood.

Before long, Jake swaggered in with a heavily inked blonde in tow. Her tattoos told a story, and when she grinned, it was like a meth-induced smile that hinted at the wild side she was riding. Delaney nodded in acknowledgment of the unspoken recognition of their shared affiliation.

"So, what's hanging, Jake? I didn't catch wind of anything going down at the Super Bowl," Delaney's tone was casual, laced with the kind of curiosity that brewed beneath the surface of the underground world they inhabited.

Jake leaned in, his demeanor exuding a mix of excitement and incredulity. "Man, you won't believe this shit. Vogel got so damn furious he offed one of his top dogs. Just put a bullet in the back of the guy's skull, right in front of his crew. Can you fucking believe that?"

Delaney's eyebrows shot up, the news hitting him like a jolt of adrenaline. "No shit?" He swigged his beer, absorbing the intensely dark situation. As Jake continued, Delaney's interest deepened. "So, out with it, Jake. What the hell was the plan for the game?"

Jake leaned back, his expression a mix of frustration and disbelief. "Word is, the Iron Eagles had the inside track. Those Chinese fuckers peddled some deadly virus to The Organization. The plan was to release the shit at the game. No one would croak right then and there, but they'd all turn into damn carriers, spreading the shit everywhere they went. Crazy as fuck, huh?"

"Damn, that's some crazy shit," Delaney muttered, shaking his head in disbelief. "Good thing none of our guys were in the mix at that game."

A flicker of realization crossed Jake's face as if he hadn't considered the ramifications for their crew. "You got a point there, man."

"Here's the kicker," Jake added, his voice dropping a notch. "Someone on the scene managed to snag an FBI chick's name. Vogel's got a damn hit out on her. She's gonna have some heavy heat on her tail, that's for sure."

The weight of the conversation hung in the air, the grim reality of their world a constant backdrop to every interaction. In this outlaw realm, where danger was the currency and alliances could be forged as quickly as they could crumble, survival meant staying a step ahead and never underestimating the stakes that came with their chosen path.

TWENTY-NINE

Lomax extended an open-ended period of leave to Jeannie following the devastating attack that left her car totaled and her home uninhabitable. However, her resilience and determination proved unyielding. She returned after just two days, unwilling to allow the malicious act to break her stride. In her heart, the burning desire to reclaim her life, even in the face of adversity, fueled her every step.

Jeannie found solace in the embrace of Delores and Walter's support as she accepted their offer of refuge. They provided a temporary haven while she navigated the tumultuous aftermath of the bombing. This respite not only allowed her to regroup but also ensured the safety of the few belongings that had miraculously survived the explosion, her cherished koi chief among them. These aquatic companions, symbolic of her resilience, held a special place in her heart, and safeguarding them became a beacon of continuity amid the chaos.

Jeannie was already back at her post within the familiar walls of her workplace just three days after the shocking ordeal. Her desire to address the loose ends from the bombing was unwavering. She delved into the aftermath with a methodical focus, overseeing the follow-up procedures she had meticulously outlined. Uncovering the nature of the virus that had been intercepted at the stadium remained a priority, one she pursued with the same vigor that defined her investigative prowess.

Another thread tugged at Jeannie's curiosity amid these pursuits. Even though the case had transitioned to an ATF jurisdiction, she couldn't ignore the lingering question about the explosive device that had devastated her property. The nature of the bomb and the culprits behind its deployment ignited a relentless drive within her.

And beyond these pressing matters, a deeper motivation smoldered beneath the surface. Revenge. A searing need to expose and bring down the individual responsible for orchestrating the attack — the very Chancellor of Germany, the elusive missing Hitler clone.

The flames of determination burned hotter than ever, and every fiber of Jeannie's being was focused on unmasking the puppeteer behind the scenes and dismantling the web of intrigue that threatened not only her life but the fabric of the world itself.

However, once again, like the hunt for the dangerous virus vials, she knew the Hitler clone was about to start World War III with his invasion of Poland. She was driven by a resolute determination in this pursuit that could not be extinguished, no matter the obstacles in her path.

Over her and Ismail's second cup of coffee in the breakroom, Lomax entered with Burk and Darcy. After telling them she was fine and had already arranged with her insurance company to start rebuilding her garage, she learned another anonymous email had just come in. Lomax read it to everyone present.

"There's another threat on the horizon," Lomax's voice carried a grave weight as he addressed his team. "This time, it's directed at Jeannie Loomis herself. The Organization is targeting her in retaliation for thwarting their terrorist scheme at the football stadium. We need to implement 24/7 security around her immediately. We can't afford any gaps in protection while we work on deciphering their next move."

Ismail's response held a touch of dark humor, an attempt to lighten the heavy atmosphere that had settled in the room. "A little late for that, isn't it? I bet your insurance agent loves you," he quipped, offering a wry smile in an effort to inject a spark of levity.

Jeannie's response carried a mixture of pragmatism and resolve. "Oddly enough, he's not too displeased. I wouldn't be surprised if he reaches out to you soon, sir, to inquire if the FBI is contributing to the rebuild and replacing my wheels," she stated, her gaze shifting toward Lomax. The implication was clear; collaboration extended beyond the confines of investigations, encompassing insurance claims and bureaucratic assistance.

Lomax's expression remained resolute, focused on the task at hand. "Jeannie, we're going to do everything in our power to keep you safe. The moment someone is on the radar, the stakes change, and we're not going to let them dictate the terms." His words carried a weight of determination, an unwavering commitment to safeguarding one of their own.

"I hate to beat a dead horse, but seriously, who is this guy?" Ismail quipped, his tone tinged with a touch of exasperation." And check out the way he writes, so damn formal," he added, his incredulity evident.

The air was tense with anticipation. Weber and Wagner were poised a little past 6 p.m., awaiting Jeannie's imminent arrival home. They had deduced her patterns through vigilant surveillance, as she daily parked her bureau car in the driveway of her temporarily unoccupied home before tending to her beloved animals. Tonight, as had become routine, she'd spend the night under her neighbor's roof.

"Once we catch those headlights, we've got to be ready to move. No time to waste," Weber's voice carried an edge of urgency, mirroring the vital nature of their task. The details had been meticulously planned: their swift exit from the vehicle, the element of surprise, and the denial of any opportunity for her to react. The knowledge that she was armed only added to the calculated speed of their operation.

"Remember, speed is crucial. We close in, take our shots, and then we're out. No second guesses," Wagner's instructions held a resolute determination, his tone indicating the ominous seriousness of their mission. His query to Weber bore the weight of a final confirmation. "You got that suppressor on, right?"

Weber's response was swift and affirmative. "Yeah, it's locked and loaded. My mask is primed, too. And speaking of our 'Führer,' you still want those post-mission snapshots on your cell phone?" The question hung in the air, a reminder of the chilling proof they were required to offer their shadowy puppeteer, the driving force behind their grim endeavors.

Twenty-one hundred yards separated Delaney from the unfolding scene involving Weber and Wagner. Armed with a Sig Sauer Electro-Optics Tango 6T 1-6x24 Ultralight Mount, Sean was positioned as if he were a silent passenger in the rear of their vehicle.

With unwavering precision in a display of expertise honed through years of training, he executed two swift and lethal head shots within a five-second span. The members of The Organization, unsuspecting and confined within their vehicle, fell victim to the calculated strike.

Their figures remained slumped in the front seats in the aftermath, forever stilled by the deadly accuracy that Sean's skill had wrought. The vehicle sat down the street from Jeannie's residence, a silent testament to the swift and decisive intervention that had thwarted the impending danger. Delaney's actions had effectively snuffed out the threat from his vantage point, an unseen hand that had reached across the expanse to safeguard the life of his ally and old lover.

Jeannie was already up and about before Delores and Walter stirred. The kitchen greeted her with a simple gesture of care — a blueberry muffin sitting on the counter accompanied by a note in Delores' familiar handwriting. The note instructed her to warm up a cup of coffee from the pot and wished her a safe and pleasant day. Heeding Delores' words, Jeannie followed the simple routine, allowing the warmth of the gesture to wrap around her.

As her coffee was heating, Jeannie took a moment to pen a grateful note in response, thanking her hosts for their thoughtfulness. The exchange carried a subtle but profound sense of camaraderie, the comfort of shared space, and support within the fabric of their friendship.

A plan took shape in Jeannie's mind as the day unfurled. She knew showing her gratitude required more than just words. She resolved to make a stop on her way back home later that evening. Her destination was a familiar patisserie that held the key to a sweet gesture of appreciation. She would buy a strawberry cream cake — Delores and Walter's favorite indulgence.

The evening would provide an opportunity to express her gratitude in person and let her friends know how much their hospitality meant to her. Their willingness to open their home during her time of need hadn't gone unnoticed. She had received a text message notifying her that she could safely return to her house while the garage was under reconstruction. It was a sign of resuming normalcy, a step towards regaining control of her surroundings.

The traffic had swelled beyond its usual congestion, and Jeannie found herself navigating a sea of crawling vehicles. Seeking a potential explanation for the gridlock, she reached out to dispatch inquiring about any accidents affecting the Dumbarton Bridge or northbound Highway 101. The response, however, was devoid of incidents; the surge in traffic was simply a result of the evening commute's volume.

"Great," she muttered under her breath, the frustration evident in her voice as she tapped into her radio's frequencies, flipping through stations in search of a reprieve. The familiar voice of her favorite conservative reporter provided a momentary distraction from the snarl of vehicles around her.

Her mood soured further as she tuned in. The reporter's accounts carried a somber tone, relaying the tension brewing along the border between Germany and Poland. The region was poised to ignite like a powder keg, and Jeannie needed no prompting to identify the one holding the metaphorical match. The Chancellor of Germany, the embodiment of the Hitler clone known as Vogel, was the provocateur steering the course towards chaos.

The news sent a chill down her spine, the weight of the global implications pressing heavily upon her shoulders. At that moment, amid the frustrating traffic and the echoes of the news report, desperate haste needed in her mission became more pronounced. Jeannie knew the shadows of history were merging with the present, and she was determined to unravel the threads that bound them, unveil the sinister designs lurking beneath the surface, and thwart the dangerous game that threatened the world's stability.

THIRTY

"Good morning, boss lady," Ismail's cheerful tone resonated as he gallantly held the door open, a gesture of respect and camaraderie rolled into one. "So, spill the beans—how's the situation with your house? And speaking of which, any plans for a new ride? If you're considering a Ferrari, you know I'm your expert tester," he added, a mischievous grin playing on his lips.

"Oh, Ferrari, huh? I had my mind set on a Lamborghini," she retorted, her impish smile mirroring the playful banter. It wasn't lost on either of them that the choice was more about whimsy than necessity; after all, they both knew she could easily acquire one of each if she wished.

The uproar echoing from the Chancellor's office resonated far beyond its closed doors. The tempest within manifested in screams that pierced the air, accompanied by the percussive rhythm of fists pounding against the desk and objects being hurled against the walls. A tumultuous display of anger and frustration was taking place.

Outside, an unspoken agreement held everyone at bay. No one dared to breach the threshold of the office, understanding the wrath that was consuming the space within. The turmoil continued unabated, a tempest that seemed relentless in its intensity.

And then, as abruptly as it had begun, the storm subsided. The screams dwindled into a silence that stretched out like a vacuum. The tension was palpable, the atmosphere heavy with the aftermath of the emotional tempest that had unfurled.

The final shout came from Vogel, "Colonel Becker, Major Hossteller, and Captain Heilderman, you stay. The rest of you, I should have you all shot. Just like my father, I have been betrayed. Get out! Get out!"

The office door swung open, revealing a tableau of high-ranking Organization officers. Their ashen faces starkly reflected the shock that had seized them. The tumultuous outburst within the room had left its mark, imprinting their expressions with a mixture of astonishment and trepidation.

Becker, Hossteller, and Heilderman stood rigidly at attention, the weight of the room's atmosphere almost unbearable. Beads of sweat traced delicate paths down their cheeks, a testament to the tension that hung heavily in the air. Vogel's outburst had left its mark, evident in the tremors that still coursed through him. His arm, weakened and unsteady, moved erratically as if detached from his control. Flecks of his saliva marked his desk in a reminder of the intensity of his emotions.

Despite his attempts to sweep his hair from his eyes, it stubbornly persisted in falling back into place, a small yet persistent annoyance amid the larger turmoil. The scene was a portrait of disarray, a reflection of the inner chaos that had consumed Vogel in his moment of rage.

He sank back into his seat, a deep inhale filling his lungs to reclaim his composure. His glasses came off in a momentary respite before they settled back on the bridge of his nose. Retrieving a rolled document from beneath his desk, his fingers traced the contours of the parchment before unfurling it, revealing a meticulously detailed battle plan for the invasion of Poland.

Vogel's voice, steady yet tinged with an air of command, sliced through the tension-laden room. " I entrust a task to you when you step out of this room. You will execute the man who holds the rank just beneath yours. Is that understood?" The directive hung heavy in the air, its weight amplified by the somber nature of the surroundings. "Eliminate your immediate subordinate," he reiterated, his words an echo of authority.

"Then," his gaze intensified, locking onto each set of eyes present, "elevate the next individual in line. Don't concern yourself with the generals; I've already orchestrated their fate." The orders flowed with cold precision in a calculated choreography of power shifts. "This is to be executed immediately," he emphasized, his tone brooking no delay or hesitation.

Vogel gestured to the map before him with a sweep of his hand, fingers indicating the amassed troops along a front. "Here, at this line," he declared, voice unwavering, "our forces will surge into Poland. Within the next 48 hours, the world will bear witness to the resurgence of the Fourth Reich." The words hung in the air like an unspoken omen, foretelling a storm of events that would reverberate far beyond the boundaries of that room.

"Jeannie," an excited voice heralded Darcy and Burk's entrance into her office. The energy was palpable as they exchanged glances, both clearly ready to deliver crucial information. "We've got the scoop on the virus they intended to unleash at the stadium," Darcy exclaimed, her tone a blend of **urgency** and discovery.

"Just as we suspected," she continued, the words tumbling out in rapid succession, "it's a weaponized variant of the Covid virus. Logical, right? I mean, anyone with half a brain knows Covid-19 originated in China, but this... this is a whole different beast. Far deadlier than the Chinese flu. The kicker? Its incubation period is 72 hours, so the infected wouldn't even realize it until they'd spread it to who knows how many others."

Burk chimed in, filling in the gaps with somber clarity, "According to the lab's assessment, the fatality rate could have topped 80%. They're scrambling to develop a countermeasure, but the echoes of the Covid-19 debacle have left many Americans wary of government interventions." His words bore a heavy weight, the realization of the uphill battle to come evident in his expression.

As they stood there, the room seemed to absorb the deeply serious nature of their findings. The clash between scientific endeavor and public trust underscored the monumental challenge ahead. It was a testament to the complex web of consequences woven by past actions, and Jeannie felt the weight of her mission deepening as the threads of danger became ever more intricate.

"Now, that's not all," Darcy's voice interjected, brimming with urgency. The room seemed to crackle with anticipation as her words hung in the air. "We just got off the line with an Interpol agent based in Brazil. He confirmed the identities of the decomposed bodies of a man and a woman. These were Vogel's biological parents. The kicker? He'd long departed the scene by the time their remains were discovered. But here's another kicker: Interpol managed to piece together the puzzle of the missing Hitler clones."

Jeannie and Ismail's attention was fully ensnared by Darcy's revelation, their anticipation palpable. Jeannie made a swift decision before they could fully absorb the information. "Hold that thought," she interjected, her determination clear. "I want Lomax to hear this. Let's get him in here."

It didn't take long before Lomax entered Jeannie's office, his presence a testament to the seriousness of the unfolding news. With a composed nod, Jeannie introduced Darcy and Burk's impending revelation, her gaze shifting to them as they began to speak.

The room seemed to bristle with tension as the words spilled forth. "Interpol managed to trace down the whereabouts of one of the missing clones," Darcy began, her tone steady despite the weight of the information. "The owner was in Berlin. However, both he and his wife met a tragic end in an apartment fire. A teenage male body was found among the remains. In Berchtesgaden, the same fate befell a family of four — the parents, a young female, and what we believe was the second clone."

A solemn silence descended, punctuated by the terrible implications of each piece of information. Lomax's voice cut through the stillness, adding a layer of sobering perspective. "So, our assumption was accurate. Doctor Hausser crafted not four but five clones of Hitler. Three were presented during that chilling ceremony on the island, while he retained the fourth for himself. The fifth clone, as we've learned, was placed in the hands of the couple whose bodies were discovered in the Brazilian jungle."

Ismail's insight added another layer of mystery to the puzzle. "The question of why Hausser created that fifth clone, or why he bestowed it upon that couple, will likely remain unanswered," he mused, his voice tinged with a sense of resignation.

A shadow passed over the room as Jeannie spoke, her words laden with the weight of jurisdictional limitations. "And as for Vogel, we find ourselves unable to apprehend him. He's well beyond our reach, probably having silenced his step-parents when he felt the time was right to embrace his assumed destiny." A hint of sadness underscored her statement, the frustration of borders and boundaries palpable.

Lomax punctuated the conversation with a dose of realism, his voice tinged with a touch of cynicism. "As for the international community, it's a familiar tune. Tough talk, minimal action. With German troops poised on the Polish border, the United Nations is likely to remain on the sidelines. Vogel holds the stage, and it seems we're all confined to watching from the wings." The resignation in his tone mirrored the complexities of a world in turmoil, a reality where action and inaction danced in a delicate balance.

Jeannie's cell phone emitted a sharp ring, the caller ID flashing Delores's name. "This can't be good," she quipped, a wry smile tugging at her lips. "It's my dear neighbor, Delores. Let's see if my house got hit again, shall we?"

The room seemed to gravitate toward her as the call unfolded. "Hello, Delores. What's going on? Oh, no. Have you contacted the police? Great. Make sure they reach out to me when they arrive. You've got my cell phone number; just let them know the FBI is on its way from our San Francisco office. Thanks a million, Delores."

Jeannie's gaze swept across the room as the call ended, her humor intact even in the face of potential trouble. "Well, folks, that was my ever-watchful neighbor, Delores. She happens to be the reigning president of our illustrious Neighborhood Alert group," she declared, her tone carrying a blend of amusement and appreciation.

A chuckle seemed to ripple through the gathered crowd as Jeannie explained the situation. "So, here's the scoop. Just a few hours after I sauntered off to work, Delores spotted a decidedly suspicious car loitering down the street from my abode. She and her valiant hubby decided to play neighborhood watchdogs, but those two mysterious fellows never budged from their vehicle."

Jeannie paused, her eyes glinting with mischief as she set the stage for a punchline. "Now, here's where it gets entertaining. These dear neighbors of mine just happen to carry concealed weapon permits. So, what do they do? They strut down the street hand in hand, armed to the teeth, and do a little investigative by peeking into that car." A grin tugged at her lips, the absurdity of the scenario evident in her expression.

"And lo and behold," she continued, her voice carrying a playful cadence, "they found not one but two gentlemen chilling out in the car sporting gunshot wounds to the head, no less. Care to take a wild guess, anyone? My money's on those fellows being part of The Organization. Oh, the joys of neighborly bonding and vigilante detective work." The room erupted into laughter, the shared moment of levity a stark contrast to the dark solemnity of their usual pursuits.

THIRTY-ONE

"Herr Doctor, tonight marks a pivotal moment in the history of the Fourth Reich," Vogel declared as Muller stepped into his office. The aura in the room was electric, charged with a sense of impending significance. Vogel's mask had been discarded, replaced by a mustache that mirrored his father's, rendering him eerily like the infamous dictator. His presence exuded an air of determination, a conviction that echoed through his words.

"Tonight, and in the hours ahead," Vogel continued, his voice resonating with a blend of anticipation and confidence, "the world will bear witness to the seismic impact of our actions. The rumble of our formidable tanks and the thunderous roar of our jets will reverberate across borders as we, once again, seize control over Poland. My father's legacy lives on through this endeavor, and I am certain he would find pride in our pursuit."

The resemblance between Vogel and his father was uncanny, a testament to the perpetuation of a legacy that held sway even across generations. Vogel's fervor was unmistakable, underscoring his belief in the path he had chosen. "But this time," he stated with unwavering resolve, "there will be no pause. Unlike my father's approach, we will not allow the world time to marshal its defenses. Once Poland is under our dominion, the momentum will only surge forward. One by one, the nations on my list will fall, the dominos of conquest toppling in rapid succession."

Vogel's gaze bore into Muller, the weight of their shared history and intertwined destinies hanging in the air. "However," he paused, his voice lowering, "this ambitious undertaking requires more than just strategy and force. It demands unwavering resilience in the face of any challenge. That's where you, my faithful doctor, play a crucial role."

Vogel's request was clear, a plea laden with a sense of dependency. "I need you to administer a potent concoction into my system, a medication that will fortify my resolve and keep my determination unshakable. I must rely on your expertise to ensure I remain resolute and unwavering, a steadfast leader, as we forge history and march toward our vision of a new world order." The intensity of his gaze communicated the serious nature of the task, the trust he placed in Muller echoing through their shared purpose.

Jeannie was home after a stressful day at work, feeling helpless as the world watched the events playing out at the border between Germany and Poland. Rumors were flying that China was supplying resources to

Germany and that Russia was also cheering Vogel's actions. She caught herself casting swear words at her TV only to notice the fish in her dining room aquarium appearing agitated by her actions and voice. She was distracted when her cell phone rang.

"Loomis," she said upon answering. No one replied. "Yes, this is Loomis. Can I help you?" Still no response. She looked at the caller ID and found it was not listed. Then, the person on the other end of the line hung up.

Jeannie quickly grabbed her gun and made sure she was not sitting by her newly installed front windows. She recognized that paranoia was setting in and rationalized it might have been a misdial. She grabbed a leftover piece of cake from the one she gave Delores and Walter and found a movie to watch.

The vast chamber buzzed with anticipation as twilight descended upon the sprawling underground bunker. High-ranking officers of The Organization, adorned in their meticulously tailored black or gray uniforms, began to stream in with their elegant spouses on their arms. The air was thick with a mixture of excitement and trepidation. The walls were draped with ominous crimson banners adorned with the black symbol of the swastika, invoking memories of a dark past.

Limousines pulled up outside the entrance, and the officers and their partners emerged, greeted by eager subordinates and echoing salutes. The attendees exchanged murmurs and nods, their eyes revealing loyalty and underlying tension alike. The atmosphere was charged with the weight of history as if the very air bore witness to the resurgence of a malevolent force.

An ornate platform had been erected in the distance. The focal point of the grand chamber, it awaited the presence of the one they all revered and feared: Chancellor Vogel, the living embodiment of their cause, the son of Adolph Hitler. This time, however, he would stand before them without the mask that had concealed his face since his ascension, and instead display his true visage that was strikingly like the one they idolized.

This pivotal juncture held dual significance; rekindling their march into Poland carried a twofold purpose. First, it would be a resounding proclamation to the world, affirming the resurgence of the Fourth Reich as a global force. Second, it would unveil his concealed persona, a reincarnation of a figure he and his devotees revered as the paramount leader history had witnessed.

Attendees snapped to attention as Vogel's car rolled to a stop. The air resounded with a deafening chorus of "Heil Hitler," a chant that sent shivers down the spine of even the most seasoned officers. Now revealed without artifice, Vogel had embraced his uncanny resemblance to the man whose legacy he sought to uphold. The newly grown Hitler mustache adorned his lip, a symbol of his commitment to his unholy mission.

Amid the fervent chants, a distant figure observed from an inconspicuous vantage point. Hidden in the shadows with his sniper rifle trained on Vogel, Sean Delaney bore the weight of history on his shoulders. The lost lives and the tarnished ideals – all of it converged in this singular moment. He knew the world could not endure another reign of terror.

With steady hands and a resolute heart, Delaney inhaled deeply and exhaled as he squeezed the trigger. A single shot pierced the cavernous silence, traveling across the expanse to find its mark. In an instant, Vogel's chest blossomed red, his eyes widening in shock and disbelief. The echo of the shot reverberated through the chamber, drowning out the chants that had celebrated his grotesque imitation.

Vogel's body crumpled to the ground, and the chant died with him. The attendees stood frozen as if time itself had halted. Reality shattered their illusion, and the truth of their leader's demise descended upon them like a hammer blow. The dream they had clung to dissipated, leaving only the bitter taste of defeat.

Delaney's presence remained unknown amid the chaos, an enigmatic figure whose act would forever remain a secret. As the Nazi flags drooped and the once-proud officers dispersed in disarray, the underground bunker bore witness to the fall of an ideology that should never have been resurrected.

COMING IN SPRING 2024

RELICS OF REDEMPTION

The Sudarium of Oviedo, a bloodstained cloth that once enveloped Jesus Christ's head after his crucifixion, has been stolen, prompting the involvement of FBI Agent Jeannie Loomis and her team in the investigation. However, they soon discover that this theft merely serves as a preliminary act for a more audacious heist: the theft of the True Cross, a fragment of the actual crucifixion cross discovered in the 4th century by St. Helena.

Jeannie becomes entangled in an intricate web of an international conspiracy, orchestrated by a clandestine organization with nefarious intentions to harness the power of the True Cross. Her quest leads her on a journey across various nations, necessitating collaboration with law enforcement agencies on a global scale.

www.ingramcontent.com/pod-product-compliance
Lightning Source LLC
Chambersburg PA
CBHW020552310726
48979CB00008B/1188/J
9798989342433